WHEN THE CICADAS STOP SINGING

ZACHARY ASHFORD

Published by Horrific Tales Publishing 2021

http://www.horrifictales.co.uk
Copyright © 2021 Zachary Ashford

A CIP catalogue record for this book is available from the British Library

ISBN: 978-1-910283-33-2

ACKNOWLEDGEMENTS

I usually dedicate my books to my wife and kids, but Ramona knows I love her and the kids know I can't wait till they're old enough to read them, so this time, I'm taking a different route.

This book wouldn't be possible without the support of Graeme at Horrific Tales. It just wouldn't. Dion, who edited this one, deserves a lot of kudos for it becoming the streamlined beast it is today, and Dan Russell's early read was invaluable.

Mostly, though, I want to dedicate this to two of my favourite bands: Revocation and The Black Dahlia Murder. If people enjoy this as much as I've enjoyed their music, I'll know I've done a stellar job.

PS. I can't not mention her. My wife, Ramona is seriously amazing. She indulges all of my obsessions and without her holding my life together while I journey into other realms, it would all fall apart. I love you, babe!

PPS. You, the reader. The fact you're holding this is pretty unbelievable to me. You rule!

WHEN THE CICADAS STOP SINGING

BY

ZACHARY ASHFORD

CHAPTER ONE

The cicadas had fallen silent. If Cora hadn't seen the lizard monster earlier, she may even have taken a moment to enjoy the peace. She could have appreciated the other sounds that symphonised the forest here beneath their white noise and gave the living foothills beneath the ridges and uprearing escarpments of the mountain its voice. But the world was a less gentle place now. To neglect this sign would be to invite the reaper back into the camp.

From her vantage point high up the track, she watched the creature, a saurian humanoid, approach. It didn't seem to matter how many times they intruded, it would always remain a stressful and sobering experience. This was life now. Precarious. Fragile. Although she was sure they must have their own unique features, she only ever saw the monster that had crept into her sanctuary and taken her boy.

The tension in her chest knotted into a clustering ball of panic as its tongue flickered in and out, no doubt tracking her scent. It tilted its head to the side, listening perhaps. If it were farther out, she'd lead it through the steel-jaw traps she'd pilfered from farmhouses and supply stores over time. This close, she could only hope to stay far enough ahead of it to get it to the murder hole where she could finish it off the old way.

Steadying herself, she took a deep breath, cupped her hands to her mouth and whooped. The sound echoed off rock-faces and travelled beneath the canopy in a swelling burst. There was a poignant moment of nothing, and then the cicadas reacted, exploding into frantic noise that washed over the forest like a tidal wave, echoing off the mountain above her. Birds erupted from trees, cawing loudly, and a kookaburra threw its head back, laughing like a maniac.

The drooling beast tilted its head to one side then swivelled robotically, dismissing the known, seeking the source of this new sound. It took several tentative steps on its long, bipedal legs, tasting the air; crouched and shat, expelling whatever rancid carrion it had last devoured, and then roared mightily.

Cora pounded her chest three times with her palm and whooped again, drawing its attention at last.

It broke into a sprint, becoming a blur of motion beyond the boughs and branches of the forest below. So did Cora. Her legs pumped like pistons, propelling her along the forest trail she knew so well. Branches whipped at her face, leaving thin scratches on her drawn cheeks, but she kept pushing on. The matted tangle of her hair blew back and the contents of her rucksack bounced and jarred with each footfall. There was, in the moment, no fear but the imminent threat sharpened her senses. She was elevated, invigorated to her highest potential. Deep breaths pumped her lungs like bellows, and as she ran, she took in the vivid aromas of the bush: gum, cedar, lantana, carrion, stagnant water, dry earth and...was that smoke? Whatever the scents were, they were fleeting, lost in the wind as her frantic sprint pushed her ever-onward. With bounding steps, she took the base of the small foothill by the water hole, and then she leapt across the narrow gulley. She pushed hard, calves burning with effort. The lizard's footfalls pounded behind her, syncopated slapping, getting closer. Its growling seemed like exhortations to slow down, to give up; it would be so easy. Her mind flew to the cairn and those horrible moments of loss played in her mind again. She snarled, shook her head and put on a spurt.

The rocky outcrop at the top of the cliff-face loomed like an uprearing head. Almost there. Cora hit the clearing like a juggernaut, ready to scramble up the narrow passage which wound its way through the ancient rock-fall to the base of the cliff.

She vaulted a fallen tree and kept running, eyes straining for the trip-wires she'd set across the goat-track. Careful. Careful. The bastard creature screeched as it closed the gap between them. Cora hopped over one, two, then sped up again. Seconds later, the fetid predator crashed to the ground, brought down by slender steel. It roared again, furious now. She dared not hope that it had tumbled awkwardly enough to injure itself.. Stopping to check could be the death of her. She would hear soon enough if the chase had resumed. And sure enough, its scuffling feet had it back up and after her within seconds, raptor claws clicking on the hard and dusty soil. The only way this contest was going to end was with blood.

Using her momentum, Cora sprinted across a stretch of bare ground, then grabbed a stubby tree branch and swung to the right, heading for the small cave and its natural chimney that provided access to higher ground. As she scrabbled for purchase she heard the bastard thing scream, thundering across the clearing. It was a sound she'd heard many times now, but it never failed to strike fear into her, taking her right back to the night she lost her boy, and those other screams of pain and terror.

She kicked and pushed her way up the rock crevice as talons whooshed through the air, sparking off the hard rhyolite surface. They'd have raked through her calf like fire through a dry forest, but she could reflect on that later. Right now, she had to reach the rocks at the top of her murder hole.

The thing's demonic braying echoed off the walls as it began its own ascent, but it was too slow. Cora had practice and a head start. She hefted one of the head-sized rocks, grunting with the effort, and threw it behind her, hoping to hit the monster unsighted. The braying was cut short with a thud.

The monster roared its pain.

9

Cora turned now, chancing a look into the abyss. The creature's burning eyes were remorseless and intent, but it was the sharp teeth, dripping thick with saliva, that gave her nightmares. She bellowed, and cast the rock down. It hit the side of the lizard's face with a sickening crack. The monster was rocked by the blow. It slid then fell to the stony ground with a meaty crunch and a hollow gasp. After a short while it tried to get back to its feet but something inside it was broken. Runnels of blood trickled down its jowls, weeping from a fist-sized crack beneath its eye. Across its scaled and naked chest, she could see the scars of past battles. Someone, at some point, had left it with a raking slash that had healed poorly into ruddy skin. Pus oozed from the wound, adding a sickening layer to its reptilian stench. Whoever had inflicted that wound must surely be dead; to have hurt it so severely and then left it alive was a madness that could not be imagined. They did not forgive or forget. Ever.

She pictured Barney, clutched in its jaws, and she hurled another stone down at the creature, then another, and another. Eventually, from beneath the half-dozen small boulders, its leg stopped twitching. The puddle of blood beneath its fractured skull continued to blossom outwards in a pretty puddle, glinting in the sunlight and, as the creature fell silent, the cicadas took up their tuneless singing once more.

Crows cawed, and the cadences of her campsite fell back into their familiar patterns. The parrots squawked. The waterfall gurgled, and the bugs buzzed and clicked. Cora climbed carefully back down the chimney and unbuckled her knife from its sheath. This was perhaps her most prized possession, liberated from an abandoned camping supplies store on the long journey out here from the city. Heavily weighted, razor sharp and a good six inches long, it cut through scaled skin and meat, gristle and bone with relative ease. She began to remove the rocks until the creature's head was revealed, crushed and sad-looking. She plunged the blade hilt-deep into the lizard's throat and ripped it across in a slashing motion. The gout of arterial blood was weak, the pressure coming from its heart already spent by the wounds she had inflicted on it.

This one too, was dead, it didn't fix anything. She was still alone, and life out here, in this treasured place she'd chosen to spend her last days in, watching the end of the world, would go on in grim solitude. She sat back against the outcrop and wiped her face with a quivering arm. Flies were buzzing around her kill and the ants, materialising from the soil with magical efficiency, had already formed a trail between their nest and the puddle of blood. A crow announced its presence in a tree nearby, but she knew it was only an observer. Not once had she seen one strip the lizards of their flesh. There was something...wrong about the creatures, and it wasn't just their extraordinary size. Whatever they were and wherever they had come - each widely debated in the early days, before the ruin - they just didn't seem to be part of this world. Nature abhorred them, though they strutted over it like landlords. She would need to burn it sooner rather than later, but as she let her breathing slow and her heartbeat calm and she wiped her tears of grief and anger away from her face, she heard the unmistakable sound of footsteps coming close. Human.

And then, a short distance away, a man and woman emerged from the forest. The man raised a gun and trained it directly on her heart.

CHAPTER TWO

With the rock-face behind her, Cora was trapped. He could shoot her before she got more than a foot up the chimney. The man was huge, looming over her like some great ox. His eyes were sharp though. Piercing and quick. A mess of straw-coloured hair, patchy and knotted, jutted from his head in tufts. His teeth were yellow and broken, and there was a rank smell. He was sick, that much was obvious. "Steady," he said, stretching the last vowel out in warning. Sunlight glinted off his scratched sunglasses, but the bulbous lenses of his aviators couldn't hide the fact his face was a mess. The skin was mottled and cracked. Sunburn or psoriasis, it was hard to tell. Something else, maybe. It peeled in flakes that caught in his stubble. His chapped lips were scabbed and scales of dried blood perched tenuously around his septum. "You handled that fucking thing pretty effectively. We need to know you're not a threat to us."

"You've got the gun," she said evenly, her eyes flicking across to the woman and back. Ever since she'd come out here, she'd been trying to eke some form of control over her own life. The cities were destroyed, uninhabitable thanks to the poisonous mists that had engulfed so much of the country, and the fucking lizards were everywhere. They'd followed shortly after the gas and had quickly set about dragging survivors from their hiding places to feast on their flesh. This was her one place of refuge. She knew it, she controlled it, her boy was here, or what was left of him. It was home. Hers. The barrel of the gun begged to differ. She'd survived out here for a long time now, but in the last few months, she'd felt that safety crumbling. There were more lizards now, for one thing. There must be slim picking left in the cities to send them out this far in search of food. Even the forest seemed more hostile in the bastard heat this summer brought. Tinder dry. And on several occasions, she'd smelled fires on the breeze. If the forest caught, it could mean the end of everything. Then again, so could this gun.

"Your knife," the man said. "Kick it over this way." He gestured impatiently then, when she failed to comply, he turned to the girls beside him. "Woman," he said, "Grab it off her."

She stepped forward quickly enough, but there was something about her gait that spoke of reluctance. Cora tried to take the measure of her as she approached. She was stick-thin and wiry, unlike the man whose physique practically boasted of protein. Beneath her lank black hair, a puffy and swollen bruise marred the hard lines of her cheek. She wasn't as dry-looking as the man, but whatever had happened to her, it had hurt. She snatched up the knife and looked down at the lizard.

"There's no need for this," Cora said. She slowly moved her feet, seeking purchase, ready to leap to the side should the man look like firing. Not that it'd do much good. "Just tell me what you want. I don't have much, but—"

"Just stay there and shut up," the man said. "You live here, right?"

She nodded.

"Thought so. What's with the cairn up there?" he asked. "Didn't look very big. Dog or something?"

That caught her off-guard. She cast her eyes down, trying to hold it together. It would be dangerous to show any weakness. She pictured her son playing. Digging in the sand by the water hole. Feeding the turtles. A sob burst out.

The woman nudged her. "Answer the question, love. It's

all right."

Cora wiped her face.

He jerked the gun as she moved.

"No sudden movements."

"Darren, enough!"

He eyeballed the woman. Turned back to Cora. "So?"

"My boy, all right? We came out here together. He— A lizard came. In the night."

"Ah, shit, I'm sorry."

"Darren, just put the gun away." The girl tugged on his shoulder. "She's not a threat, can't you see that? Let's just do what we need to and leave her be."

He spat onto the fallen leaf-litter beneath a patch of nearby shrubbery then scratched the tip of his peeling nose, thinking it through. At last, he pushed his glasses up onto his crown and revealed his eyes. They were bloodshot and puffy. "It's a tense first impression," he said, "but it's for the best. People are pricks these days. We wouldn't want unnecessary conflict."

The barrel of the gun still filled Cora's world. "Are you gonna let me up? We need to burn it."

He holstered the pistol. "TV called them lizards. You around for that?"

"Yeah, I caught that part."

He spat again, wiping saliva from his chapped mouth. "Sarah, go and get the food off the fucking fire. We'll drag the lizard down there."

"I have a place," Cora said. "Close by. We'll take it there, dig a fire-pit and cover it up."

"What's all this 'we' business? I'll be digging fuck-all for you." He snarled, revealing his rotten chompers once again. There were more than a few gaps.

The girl returned, her eyes darting about wildly. "You need a hand?"

The big man shook his head, laughing. "Well, look at Little Miss Cub Scout." His lip curled into a mocking sneer. "Someone's mighty keen to build a bridge, ain't she? Don't worry about it, woman. She's just scared of getting lizard-bits in the water. I say we sit back and enjoy the show."

"You're a bloody asshole."

He stopped smiling then and glared. The bruise on her face was no mystery, but the woman – Sarah – met his eyes with a sneer of her own.

Cora, stuck out a hand and stepped forwards to break the tension, forcing the man to shake it. "Look, I get that you need to be sure people are safe, but we're all good now. I'm Cora. It's good to meet you both." She didn't know which way this was going to go but she'd rather avoid violence if possible. Shaking his hand was a good way to shut that possibility down, though it turned her stomach to touch him. She could feel how dry his palms were. How rough and cracked the skin, like a dried-out salt-pan. "How did you find your way here?"

He snorted. "That's none of your business. We're passing through, but this is a pretty good set-up you've got here. Might impose on you for a bit."

"Darren, we've got everything we need on the boat."

He turned again, shaking his head. "Why the fuck would we empty the basement when this bitch is loaded to the gills? You saw the set-up she's got. Fucking tools, fishing line, fruit...and you want to eat our canned shit while we wait. No thank you."

Cora felt a cold chill run through her. They'd been in her camp. When? Had they really only just arrived, or had they been here for longer? Watching her. Waiting for their opportunity.

"You're being an asshole."

"Nah, fuck that. A few nights on land will be good for the legs. They need a stretch. Besides, we're already halfway up this big bastard. Why would we go all the way back?"

The girl, Sarah, pursed her lips and Cora wondered again just what had brought them here. She pulled a short length of rope, already lassoed at one end, and secured it on the lizard's legs before rolling the rest of the boulders off.

"You two can work out your story while I get this started."

Darren reached out and snatched the rope. "Gimme that. Can't have you showing me up in front of my girl now, can I?"

He hefted the lizard up and over his bullish shoulder. "Lead the way."

CHAPTER THREE

The campground had once been a place of mirth and recreation, but liana vines, ferns and groundcover had stretched across the old common area like groping hands; a carpet of nature reclaiming the land humanity had stolen. There was scant sign of the small personal campfires enjoyed by recreational campers before the ruin. Most had been washed away or covered in soil by wind and rain. There were, however, the dilapidated remains of two campground barbecues, their bricks cracked and covered in fungi, grills rusted beyond repair. Cora's old fire pit rested nearby. She burned things here whenever she needed to; lit good-sized fires on cold days. Farther on, beyond a low line of ferns and balga plants, stood Barney's cairn. She'd put it somewhere he'd loved to play, overlooking the creek down below. She had known this campsite from her youth. Memories of it lit up her soul. She had first come here on a school camp and then many times after that with friends, and then, eventually, after the city fell. Barney's resting place was the sun she revolved around now. It anchored her, warmed her, kept her going in these darkened days.

She lengthened two sides of the fire pit with her makeshift shovel, breaking away the soft soil. Next, she laid the framework for a strong fire with a lattice of thick branches. Cora didn't expect them to help, but she could have done without the obnoxious comments telling her how she should be doing it.

Eventually, the girl came forward with a lighter as Cora placed tinder at the base. "Here you go. Least we could do."

No point wearing down good flint when she didn't have to. Cora dropped the tool back into her pocket and accepted the lighter: a scarred and beaten Zippo. Someone had broken the safety feature off the wheel so it was easier to spin. She tested it and nodded. "Thanks."

Darren began to chant. "It only takes a spark to get a fire going." He laughed hard and made a crude gesture to Sarah. The woman just scowled at him, so he continued. "Soon all those around can warm up in its gloaming." Abruptly, he stopped singing. "Well, come on then, what are you waiting for? Light the bloody thing."

Cora rolled the wheel and held the flame to the tinder. It ignited and before long, the bundled fuel beneath the framework was burning like a furnace. Together, she and Sarah lifted the dead monster and draped it over the fire. Tendrils of flame licked up at the creature with wickedly forked tongues, and a meaty aroma soon filled the camp. "Jesus. Smells good enough to eat, doesn't it?" Darren flicked a pebble at Sarah. "Hey. Did you get those beans off the other fire?"

"You know I did."

"Why the blazes am I still hungry then? Have we eaten them already or did I just forget about it?" He grinned at Cora as if he'd said something particularly witty.

The girl rubbed her forehead and rose from the termite-eaten log that served as a bench. "You said to get them off the fire so they wouldn't burn."

"Don't tell me what I said, woman. Go and get 'em. I'm hungry as a turkey on Tuesday." Darren shook his head and tutted dramatically as she headed for their tent. "Bloody women, eh?"

Cora pretended not to notice as Sarah walked off to get the food.

"I said the bloody thing smells good, love. It's a shame

to let meat like that burn and spoil." He rubbed his stomach.

"I wouldn't eat it if I were you."

"You would, though. If you were starving." He flicked a little stone into the fire. Sparks and smoke plumed where it landed. The embers around it glowed. "You know you would; little girl-scout like you. Waste not, want not."

"In fact," Cora said, "it's high time we moved away from this smoke. No telling what's in it."

"You're bloody soft, you are. There's nothing in that smoke. Just good meat turning to cinders. What do you eat around here anyway? You've got to have something stashed away."

"This forest is my food supply. I knew a guy who taught me about the bush. Showed me what I could and couldn't eat."

"I'll bet he did. Open wide, eh?" His comment got no traction so he tried another tack, determined to get a rise out of her. "Oh, I get it. You're one of those people. Living like an old coon, eating witchetty grubs and shit. Thinks it brings you closer to nature. Should have known. No wonder Sarah seems to like you; her grandpa was one of 'em."

A finger of annoyance caught on Cora's spine. "You know, Sarah was right. You don't have to stay. All things considering, I think I've been pretty tolerant so far. Why don't you keep opinions like that to yourself? Or go back to your boat, maybe?"

"You sanctimonious little bitch." Darren rose and closed the gap between them. "I'll stay here as long as I want to and there's nothing you can do about it." He spat at Cora's feet. "You'll be lucky if I don't take what I want and burn you in that fucking fire." He reached down to his hip and Cora saw a moment of confusion flicker across his eyes as he patted there. She had the absurd thought he was looking for his keys, but no. Not keys.

She stepped forward, steely-eyed and snarling, unwilling to give him the time to think. The high nasal pinch of his halitosis was repellent, but there could be no weakness. Any sign of it and he'd go for her. Where the hell was the gun and why had she left her knife by the campfire? "Take your things and go. You don't need to be here."

Returning with two aluminium camping plates of food, Sarah bustled in to position herself between them. "What the hell is going on here?" The heady aroma of the roasting lizard was cloying as it burned to blackness.

Cora took the opportunity to head back to the fire-pit to grab the knife, as Sarah grilled Darren with clenched teeth and sharp whispers.

"Ah, it's nothing, babe. Leave it be. The girl-scout over here was just telling me about her coon mate. Taught her how to be a bush-tucker man or something." Darren raised his voice to reach Cora. "Didn't he, darl? Taught you to eat witchetty grubs and tree bark like a proper native."

Cora snatched up the pig-sticker and faced him with a cool gaze. "Remember what I said. You don't need to be here. Camp tonight if you want, but you should climb the mountain tomorrow and do what you need to. Then keep on moving." She left him to chew on that.

There was a shuffling of feet behind her and a bit of a scuffle, but Sarah told Darren to calm down and eat. "Whatever the problem is, this shit keeps happening to us. It's not her causing it."

Cora smiled grimly at that as she walked out of the camp. She wasn't entirely alone, then. The forest darkened around her as the sun moved behind the saddled peak of the mountain on its journey to the horizon. The buzz of the cicadas rose in volume. Mosquitoes whined overhead and the bushes rustled with the sounds of small mammals foraging for food. Accompanying it all was the rush and gurgle of the swimming hole's waterfalls and cascades.

In her time of solitude here, she'd made various bases and storage-huts around the mountain's foothills. One would suffice as a refuge tonight. With any luck they'd be gone by the time she returned.

In recent months, she'd taken to sleeping in a shack near the waterhole. It sat just above the waterfall on a separate ridge, safe from the threat of flash-flooding. Hypothetically, she'd be able to see any lizards—or people —coming up the old track from a long way off. Right now, her biggest concern was whether anything of importance was missing. She didn't have much from her old life, but there were some small things she couldn't give up. A box holding some of Barney's baby teeth, a lock of his hair and her old engagement ring held particular value. Even that relationship had been eroded by the passage of time.

She checked for the box as soon as she reached the hut, a primitive structure built into the space between several spotted gums. She'd done her best to thatch a roof from reeds and palms, layering it with an old tarpaulin she'd rescued from a pile of rubbish, but it leaked pretty badly in the rain. Nothing had been taken, she was relieved to discover. Not from here anyway. If they'd stumbled upon it, they'd been careful – and that didn't fit the pair as she'd come to know them. She had needed to know that nothing was out of place. That she still had somewhere to call her own. This forest, this mountain was her home. She wouldn't be driven from it, or from Barney.

CHAPTER FOUR

Loading her pockets with macadamia nuts and a few strips of dried kangaroo meat, Cora sought higher ground and a bird's-eye view of the camping spot below. From the secluded spot above the waterfall, Cora could hear them drinking. By the sound of his obnoxious waffling, he was far more likely to black out than to start a second batch of trouble, but the night was young. There was still time for more bullshit. She'd half-expected Darren to try and claim her bed in a brainless attempt at exerting control over the camp, but the intruders had eventually pitched their own tent.

Cora's small fire was low enough to be hidden from the camp below, though a watchful eye might spot the flickering shadows it threw. During storms, the pit she knelt in was filled by natural runnels of storm-water and flushed over the precipice to the waterhole down below.

The low fire crackled and a bug ran desperately along the edge of a stick protruding from the flames, forced from its home within. Cora leaned in and gently caught the bug, saving it from the fire. The braying from below quietened down at last, sinking into murmurs. Cora slipped away from the fire, closer to the edge and strained to catch their conversation.

Darren asked something, low and urgent. Sounds of hurried rummaging. Frustration. It was impossible to make out exactly what was being said, but there was a rising tone of aggression. Then the girl buzzed something back at him. Darren's drunken anger won over and his next words silenced the forest around him, as though it had stopped to gasp. "Get the fucking thing back here now. Jesus Christ, woman!"

Sarah flicked her fingers apart, palms towards him –
whatever – and moved towards the water. She stooped at a
patch of weed, reached in and retrieved a bundle of old
cloth. Darren threw something at her as she returned,
cradling it gently. The projectile smashed on the ground at
her feet. An empty spirit bottle? "Hurry up, bring it here."
The forest was beginning to resume its song. A bird call
here, a low hum of cicadas there.

Sarah weighed the bundle in her hands; she flicked back
the top layer of material and examined the object inside.

"You wish, bitch. Just bring it here before that little
native wannabe comes out of the shadows with a spear or
something." He was drunk. Very drunk, The slurring spoke
volumes, but he still cut a menacing figure as he staggered
into the clearing to meet the girl. The sheer bulk of the
man, coupled with his spitefulness, made him dangerous in
any situation. He yanked the shapeless clump from her and
flung the wrapping to the ground. "Now who owns this
place?"

"Put the fucking thing away, Darren. You'll end up
hurting yourself." She tugged at his elbow. "Come on, I'll
take you to bed."

He pointed the gun at her and licked his chapped lips.
"Imagine if you were her. I'd kill you right now. Just like
those other fuckers."

"Fat lot of good that did."

He spun, pointed the gun into the mass of trees on the
other side of the waterhole. The blast echoed off the gorge
and out through the forest. It was the most jarring thing
Cora had ever heard, a promise of death and destruction. A
rock wallaby darted away from the sound in skittish panic,
and Darren drew a bead. His hand was shaking too much.
He lowered the weapon.

"What are you doing?" Sarah shoved him, furious. "If
there are any more of those things out there, or people

26

looking for us, you've just told them where we are."

He laughed. "If they can track that, then bloody good luck to 'em." He stretched an arm around her shoulder.

"And what if they've found the boat?"

"Fuck 'em. Let's go to bed."

Cora sat back. She didn't want to hear any more.

A fungus on one of the branches in the fire sizzled as the moisture inside it boiled. She poked another branch into the flames, watched it catch, breathed in deeply. The smoke smelled of eucalypt, sharp and invasive. Cora fanned it away, coughing gently. She tried to grasp some positive in what she'd just seen. Sarah was smart – much smarter than the caveman who had brought her here – and she was right about the reptiles. Any lizard close enough to hear the gunshot would be on its way. But it was the people they'd mentioned that she really wanted to know about. He'd killed someone, and he was itching to kill again. As if their own intrusion of her home hadn't been bad enough, there was now the potential for more.

But she knew where the gun was now. Having it accounted for helped, but she didn't like the fact that Darren had it. There was no doubt he would use it. He probably would have killed her already if Sarah hadn't secreted it away. She knew her man alright.

There was only one solution.

CHAPTER FIVE

The hatchet hammer in her shack was designed for breaking up firewood and driving in tent-pegs, but it would serve a different purpose tonight. She felt the weight of it in her palm. What she was about to do reminded her of *Lord of the Flies*: the scene where Jack's savages raided Ralph and Piggy's camp for the glasses. She wasn't after his sunnies though; she wanted his gun. Assuming the role of Jack in this parallel was discomforting, but she consoled herself with the fact Darren was in no way akin to Ralph. He was too mean, too violent. If he was anyone, he was Roger. Had to be. Cora's own innate moral compass had been something she'd pondered for a while now. How could she, in the face of all that had happened, retain that fundamental idea she was good? She'd fought hard to instil those principles in Barney, but to what purpose? Did her old-fashioned sense of right and wrong even have a place in the world anymore? If a vile man died in the woods, did it make a difference? Would it change her? She foraged and lived like an animal. Was she less than human now? Did animals agonise over their kills? She didn't think so, but the idea that she could be losing something so ingrained – that veneer of civilisation – was deeply troubling.

She dropped the hatchet hammer into her belt. Maybe she could knock him out, take the gun? That would put her back in control. She didn't want to give in to the savagery that could come with the compulsion to survive.

She snuck down the trail from the upper campsite, sticking to the bushes, moving slowly, creeping like an animal. From Darren and Sarah's tent came the unmistakeable sound of drunken snoring against a backdrop of cicadas and rustling undergrowth. A small snake, thin and wiry, weaved its way across the path, and it slipped into the bushes. She listened for evidence that

Sarah, too, was asleep and moved into the campsite proper, taking a position behind some shrubs. She paused and listened again.

A pale circle of torchlight appeared and pressed against the interior canvas of their tent then slid towards the door. Cora froze.

More snoring.

It was the girl. The circle of torchlight slid off the canvas, but the tent still glowed faintly. The zip of the tent rose slowly, ascending in small increments so as not to attract attention.

Cora hoped Sarah wouldn't come this way, and that she didn't need something as awkward as the bathroom. Her own situation was precarious; she was hidden, but it wouldn't take much to spot her. Any attempts to get better concealed would only make more noise. She kept her breath low and even, and tried to slow her hammering heart.

Sarah came out of the tent. Silhouetted and distorted by darkness, she checked over her shoulder, inched the zip down and strode off towards the waterhole.

Watching her leave, Cora considered the bulge under the girl's singlet then snuck across the clearing to the tent. The snoring continued unabated. She could kill Darren in his sleep and end the standoff right now. All she had to do was cut his throat. It would be easy. One slash, some gurgling noises and it would all be over. She fumbled for the hilt of the knife, imagining the fountain of blood, panic rising in her chest. No, she wouldn't do that. Couldn't do that.

Sarah was easy to track. She had moved briskly, leaving footprints like breadcrumbs. Cora carefully trailed them until she heard gentle thudding. Torchlight was visible ahead. Sarah was crouched, digging in the foliage a few metres off the path, just underneath a distinctively splintered tree.

Cora waited, concealed, until Sarah scurried towards the campsite, the gun buried in its shallow grave. Once she was sure the girl wasn't coming back, Cora retrieved the bundle. The gun rested inside the cloth, along with a small box of bullets. The thing was matte black, ominous, and it had the number 22 inscribed on its side. She hoped to hell the safety was on. She didn't know enough about guns to be sure. When she pressed a button on the side of the handle, the magazine released. It was full, minus four bullets. She tipped them out and placed them in her bag, along with the box of shells. Then she rewrapped the gun and buried it once more. Finally, she made her way back to the upper campsite, pausing only to squirrel the ammunition in a hollow near her hut.

CHAPTER SIX

Cora forced herself to rise at dawn. She couldn't see the black bags under her own eyes, but as she made her way down to the waterhole she could feel the weight of them. The nocturnal birds had returned to their nests and the diurnal creatures of the forest were going about their own business. Water dragons and skinks basked on sun-dappled rocks; dragonflies darted across the water, concentric ripples spreading across the surface in their wake; and finches and kookaburras laughed as the earliest tendrils of another blazing hot day crept through the foliage. Cora's favourite, though, was a freshwater turtle she saw every morning. She'd named it Maturin, and she loved to watch it cruise around the shallow banks of the swimming hole, kicking up clouds of swirling sand in the crisp water while it snatched at grubs and tiny fish. Over time, Cora had won its trust with small chunks of meat and now it would happily take them from her hand whenever proffered.

It was her routine to watch the creature while boiling her morning tea and preparing breakfast, usually eggs or nuts harvested from an abandoned macadamia farm nearby. This morning it was eggs.

She'd talked up her bushcraft to Darren, but she only used that when pressed. Food was the main reason she left the forest, security being the other—checking for signs of travellers or salvageable items on the mountain road. She was almost thankful that people had spread across the land in the decades before everything went to shit, transforming it in their dedication to survival, comfort, and progress. Without those tokens of agrarianism, she may well have starved long ago.

As it stood, she had been toying with the idea of building a chicken coop near her campsite. Chickens still roamed and roosted in the abandoned farms and she had tried once before, in the early days, to keep a few. Maintaining the coop and dealing with the increase in snakes – inevitable in this wild place – proved too much of an inconvenience at the time. The carpet snakes the chickens themselves attracted weren't much of a problem, but brown snakes were another matter.

The morning she'd come face to face with one had taught her a simple lesson: she had been moving down an embankment towards one of the creeks feeding the river, when she'd heard the unmistakable sound of a snake in motion. Whereas skinks scampered, snakes made a swishing sound. On this occasion, her angle had meant she'd met the snake at eye-level, and it had reared up into an 'S' shape, revealing the pink blotches on its creamy belly. Her heart stopped, but it looped backwards and disappeared. That morning she learned she was a natural when it came to the long jump, albeit in reverse. She got soaked but at least she was safe. Deep down, she knew the snake probably felt the same, but the point remained: the world may be full of monsters, but there's no need to invite trouble.

Cora heard Sarah and Darren's tent open as she placed the tinder and blew on the embers of last night's fire. The man's snoring still loomed heavy within. Sarah came out, arms folded, hair loose and messy. She didn't look to have slept at all. "Thought I heard you," she said.

Cora couldn't help but wonder when exactly the girl was referring to. "Hope I didn't wake you."

Sarah waved a hand dismissively. "With that noise in there?"

Cora dipped the pot into a babbling part of the water hole where the water ran fresh and clean between two boulders. "Cup of tea?"

"Seriously?" She screwed up her face. "He's not wrong

about you being set up here, is he?"

"It's hard work, but it makes life worth living." She dug into her bag and pulled out a little box. "I'd prefer a stale coffee myself, but beggars can't be choosers. Stale tea was all they had at the old chook farm."

Sarah sat on the log by the fire. The bruise on her face was a vivid purple in the soft morning light. It looked sore. She saw Cora looking and touched it defensively. "It's not what you think."

"It's none of my business." Cora averted her eyes and placed a metal frame in the fire for the pot to sit on. "I've got eggs if you want some."

"No. But thank you; we've got food. No meat left, but it's crazy how many tins of soup and shit are still around."

"Whatever you say." Cora dipped a finger in the water and wiped it on her shirt. It was almost ready.

"Is that where you were when we got here yesterday? Gathering food?"

"Pretty much."

"Can't be easy living out here." She pointed to the steps at the foot of the path by the waterhole. "Always needing to find food; always needing to be alert."

Cora took the bubbling pot off the heat and poured some of the water into a dirty old mug. It was a trap she couldn't afford to fall into: trusting the girl. Just because she was playing nice, didn't mean she was safe. Cora let the question hang. "You have a mug?" she asked instead.

Sarah nodded and went to get it.

Cora cast her gaze to the water's edge. Maturin was there, floating in the shallows, his head a small black kite just about protruding. "Hey buddy, how you doing?" The turtle watched her suspiciously as she approached, stopping right at the lip of the lapping water. "I've got

35

nothing for you this morning. You're on your own."

"Who you talking to?" Sarah had returned.

"No one." The turtle was one of her few connections left with the real world. Her mother had always loved them. She kept them in the ponds she spent so much time tinkering with. It was always there for her, and she was there for it. There was comfort in that. The turtle ducked under the water at Sarah's approach, and Cora found herself relieved. Hungry people would go to great lengths to keep themselves fed; even if the girl could be trusted, she didn't want Darren to find the little bugger.

"You talking to yourself?"

"Kinda. Got that mug?"

Sarah handed it over and the two of them sat down on opposite sides of the small cooking fire.

"He's still asleep?"

"It'll take him a while to sleep this one off." She blew on her tea. "For what it's worth, I'm sorry about all this shit."

Cora raised her eyes from her own tea to meet Sarah's. Her father had been a stubborn man who had taught that accepting apologies gave tacit approval. It practically justified the wrong action in the first place. She didn't want this apology, and she certainly didn't want one on behalf of someone else. She blew on her tea and let the silence work on Sarah.

"It's complicated...why we're here." Sarah scratched her chin, slowly, pondering. "But it's not right that you should suffer for it." She rested her mug down on the sandy ground of the clearing and held Cora's gaze. A crow cawed in a nearby tree. "He's dangerous."

"I gathered that when he fired the gun."

"I'll do what I can to keep him from hassling you, but you don't want to piss him off. He's not been himself lately."

She took a sip of her tea. "I've put the gun somewhere safe. He's not gonna like it, so stay out of his way today."

"Is that going to come back on you?" Cora swallowed the last of her own tea and flicked the dregs on the fire.

"Perhaps, but he won't really hurt me." She fingered the bruise on her face again. "This weren't his doing, just so you know. But if he had the gun and half an excuse, he'd kill you, make no mistake. He's always been a bit rough, but this is different. He's been more unpredictable lately. Snaps really easily."

"Sounds like you should take a break from him too."

"I can live with bruises. I can't watch him kill again though."

"Again?"

"Like I said, he's dangerous." She chewed her lip. "This shit's none of your business, but look, I'm giving you a fair warning. Clear out today. Just stay out of his way."

"That bad?"

"You don't want to be here." A water dragon scurried across the clearing. It stopped and bobbed its head happily before darting into the water and swimming over to a half-submerged log.

"And if me being here helps you?"

Sarah barked a laugh and flicked a rock into the fire. "Girl, I could wipe the floor with you. You won't help any. You're lucky you got away with it yesterday."

She pictured the big man's cracked skin. His chapped lips. "What's wrong with him?"

Sarah's eyes narrowed. "What do you mean?"

"His face. He looks sick, like he's got a skin condition or something."

Sarah snorted. "Suppose he should go to the doctor's and get that shit checked, eh? Maybe get some lotion for it." She inhaled sharply. "He's fine. Just stay out of his way. We'll move on as soon as I can make him."

"Before I go, tell me one thing: is he eating them?"

"Eating what?"

"The lizards."

The girl looked at her like she was out of her mind. "You don't quit do you? I already told you where he's been getting the food."

"It's important, Sarah. If he's been eating them, we could all be in danger. I've...I've heard of shit happening after that."

Sarah puffed her chest out. "A lot of shit happened in the early days, and a lot of shit was talked about it. I don't suppose you've seen too many folks since then though, am I right? So what the hell do you know? Since I've been back with him, I can account for everything he's eaten, and it's all from cans and the occasional bit of fishing or hunting."

"But?"

"But I've only been with him a few days. Before that, I can't honestly tell you."

She wondered about their backstory, but figured that right now, that would derail this train of thought. "He hasn't said anything?"

"About eating lizard monsters? Only what I heard him say to you, and if you know him, you'll know he was just trying to get a rise out of you." She stood up. "Anything else? You sure you don't wanna know where I've been, how I hooked up with him? Because it's none of your fucking business."

Cora gave her a curt bow of the head. "I need to go and set my traps and snares." She rubbed her forehead as she left, then turned. "Sarah, really—are you gonna be okay?"

"Yep." The girl tipped out the last of her tea.

"Even if he hits you?"

Sarah hocked a loogie and spat it into the bushes. "Give us the space we'll need this morning. I'll do everything I can to get us out of here by tomorrow or the day after." She walked back to the tent, unzipped it and joined the snoring Darren once more.

Down at the water's edge, the turtle had resurfaced. Cora realised she hadn't even cooked the eggs. "Looks like neither of us are eating this morning, mate."

CHAPTER SEVEN

Cora had snares and traps all over the mountain. Mostly she caught rabbits and wallabies, but occasionally, when game was otherwise scarce, she would trap a wild pig. That was always a risky business. The big ones were a nightmare to take down and even the smaller ones could be dangerous, with their sharp little tusks. The fact they never went down without a fight increased the chances of injury, and in turn, infection. Antibiotics weren't exactly lying around the place. As a result, most of her diet came from the yabbies and fish she caught in the freshwater streams around the mountain. Coupled with her small vegetable gardens and stocks of non-perishables, it had proven to be a survivalist's dream. Not that it was easy living. Every day brought its challenges and, of course, she had to remain vigilant for any lizards that might have caught her scent.

The jaw traps she still had in supply were kept in a leeside concavity in a ridge of granite that jutted from the ground like a retaining wall. The first beads of sweat had already formed on her forehead by the time she slung one over her shoulder, figuring an extra trap near the entrance to the mountain path would be a good idea. Cool wet patches bloomed from where her bag straps rested on her shoulders. The bag pressed against the small of her back, the jaw trap clinking against its buckles as she moved.

There were rabbit warrens down by the creek. A prime hunting spot. She'd often had success trapping the holes with simple nets. She preferred to fish from a small kayak that she'd found on one of the commercial campsites not far from the mountain, but she'd had some success with baited hooks she left hanging from a tree: a few barramundi, a couple of catfish. Not the best eating, but they felt like a treat when her traps let her down.

Over time, she had stocked a sensible collection of camping, fishing and hunting equipment from the nearest village and its surrounds. This area had been the starting point for a lot of outdoor adventurers, back before the ruin. It was the kind of mountain you'd find on a postcard, particularly when the sun bowed behind it in the evening and the sky turned that hazy mix of pinks, reds and purples. Its waterfalls, creeks, trails and swimming holes were hidden jewels waiting to be discovered. The major creek fed a nearby river and it was at that spot Cora had her most successful fishing trips. It was also most likely there that Darren and Sarah had moored their boat. She would need to lay eyes on that soon.

More pressing, though, was the rabbit in her snare. Its fur was a matted grey with white patches on its feet and chin, and its twitching struggles were feeble. It had clearly been there a while. Cora was fine with catching and killing wildlife for food, but she didn't like to cause suffering. Not if it could be helped. She grabbed the creature by the back of the neck and wrung it quickly. The animal shuddered once, twice, then became still. Cora slipped it into her bag. She could bleed the poor thing back at camp.

There were a couple of red claws in one of the yabby traps. One would make good eating. It was close to full-grown and would boil nicely. Cora placed it in an old, cracked lunchbox she carried for just this purpose and tossed the other one back. About a stone's throw down the creek from there was a deep black pool where mosquito larvae wriggled in their multitudes. It gathered under the roots of a huge fig with a hollow in the trunk.

Cora found herself filled with a tense anxiety she hadn't felt since her youth. She'd been brought up to be honest, even to a fault. Stealing their ammunition went against those teachings, but there was no way she could let them keep it. The idea of facing that cavernous black barrel again was terrifying, but that wasn't the only reason. She'd seen lizards listening, cocking their heads to distant sounds she couldn't detect. If there were any of the monsters in the area, they would have heard it, and it only took one of the bastards to change everything. No. Far better to remove the threat. If Darren and Sarah had to find shells in some other place far away from here, then all the better.

The hairs on the back of her neck stood on end. If Darren found out what she was doing, there was no telling how he'd react. A weapon like that in the hands of someone so clearly unhinged...? It didn't bear thinking about. She checked over her shoulder and surveyed the area to make sure she wasn't being observed, then she pulled out the stolen ammo and stuffed it all into the hollow. This could spell trouble, but it did even things up a bit.

She sat then, and watched the larvae wriggle until her nerves steadied. Farther off down the track, she heard shouting. Indecipherable but angry in tone. Cora took a deep breath, pushed herself up and continued her rounds. She climbed one of the mountain's foothills, ears cocked, listening to the wind rustling the leaves. At the top of this particular foothill, the breeze was often powerful and refreshing. It channelled through the rugged valley and came over the crest of the hill like a wave breaking on a sandbank. Cora wiped sweat from her brow and enjoyed the rushing air.

She headed off the track then into an area frequented by rock wallabies. She had seen a wallaby trap at the museum once and she'd made a few rudimentary attempts at them up here, with mixed success. They were a tool best used in groups, chasing the wallabies along the trail towards them. Today, once again, they were empty, though there was plenty of wallaby scat in the area. Ah, well. She would check again tomorrow.

She moved on and planted her jaw trap under a patch of herringbone fern at the entrance to the old walking trail, and with the sun high in the sky, figured it was almost time to head towards home, the waterhole.

Anxious as to what she might find when she got there,

she shielded her eyes and squinted at the mountain's peak, wondering if Darren and Sarah were on their way towards it, hoping to achieve whatever it was they had to do. Before she could do that, though, she had one last stop to make. The boat. She had to know just how boldly it advertised this part of the mountain to any others who would pass by as they travelled this ancient land.

She followed the main creek towards the winding bend of turgid water that passed for a river, toiling its slow way out to sea. From time to time, she had heard boats moving across it, just as she would still occasionally hear trucks and motorbikes on the highway. It felt good to know there were still people out there, she'd just prefer they keep their distance. She could see it now, as she rounded a shoulder of rock. A two-storey houseboat with a cabin and mezzanine level encircled by an outer deck. No doubt they had taken it from one of the many pontoons that still dotted the river. The days of river-cruises were long past, of course.

Seeing it sitting there, rolling gently on the lapping waves, she fought the urge to investigate. Exploring it would do her no good. She wouldn't be stealing it and leaving, and she wouldn't be taking anything from it, so what was the point. For now, all she could do was hope that it—and its two passengers—were gone in the next couple of days. Until then, she would have to hope no one else saw it. She didn't need the fact people were here advertised, and she certainly didn't want her own visibility enhanced.

When she finally returned, it was to an oppressive quiet. She hung the rabbit to bleed then cooked the red claw, but it was dread, not hunger that tightened her stomach. The whole place felt tainted. Wherever Darren and Sarah were now, their presence remained, toxic and heavy. She squinted up at the peak of the mountain, wondering if they'd begun the ascent. It was hard to tell from this angle, but she thought she saw smoke, thin and hazy.

An hour or so later, as the sun began to disappear behind the craggy ridges of the mountain's upper haunts,

Cora heard something heavy coming down from the top of the gorge. She jerked her head up, ready to fight or flee from a lizard. Darren appeared, glowering down on her from his vantage point.

With any luck the bastard will fall from the precipice and break his neck, Cora thought. Instead, he stomped down the trail, licking his chapped lips, glaring at her all the while – a hateful monster in a man's skin. He was hot, sweaty, and exhausted, but rage gripped him. "You thieving little bitch." He wrenched a branch out of his way and it catapulted back behind him, scattering leaves and seedpods across the ground. Cora whipped the knife from the ground near the cooking fire and held it in warning before her.

"Darren, cut your shit," Sarah said, coming down behind him. "We discussed this."

"Stay out of it, woman!" He reached for one of the fist-sized rocks that ringed the fire; the cracked flesh on his wrists and knuckles looked sore and inflamed. "Drop the knife, you cowardly little bitch."

Cora moved closer to the water's edge. If he charged, she could try to evade him, shove him in, maybe. The water would hopefully slow him down. "What the fuck is your problem?" she asked.

Darren threw the rock, narrowly missing her forearm. "Don't play smart with me. You know." He snatched up another straight away. She could see the peeling skin on his face giving way to a rancid yellow-green flesh beneath. He was rife with necrosis or infection or...something. If her suspicions were true – and Cora prayed that they weren't – things could get a lot worse.

"Darren," said Sarah, stretching his name to regain his attention. "She doesn't have the gun, you silly prick. I do."

His simmering rage boiled at her betrayal. "You what?" He threw the next rock at her feet. "What the fuck for?" He advanced on her. "Give it back to me."

"I will. When we're done here." She stood tall and confident, but her voice betrayed her anxiety. The bones of her clavicle stood out in silhouette in the afternoon light.

He struck her then. Savagely. "You get it and you bring it to me. Now."

Lips pursed, she jutted her chin towards him. Defiant. "No. This ain't you, Darren. You've changed. I thought you were tougher than this; you don't need it."

He stopped at that, wavering. Weakening. "I do need it. We need it." He pointed to the top of the mountain where the smoke rose, clearer now, a thin black column climbing into the sky. "There are others who'll be able to see that too."

"It's safe where it is. I'll fetch it back for you when we leave. Tomorrow, if you like. There's nothing holding us here."

"And if they come?" He pointed south. "Or the fucking lizards?"

"It ain't happening, Darren. You'll have to deal with it." She walked down the track, heading towards the boat probably. Cora was grateful for that. She saw just how well Sarah knew him. She was nimble, that one.

Darren scowled at Cora then called out after Sarah, stumbling along in her wake. For a moment, he seemed almost human; confused and weakened by indecision.

One by one, Cora collected the rocks Darren had thrown and replaced them in the ring around the fire. She could still hear him calling after the girl when Maturin's black head popped up. Cora gave him the thumbs-up. "Never mind us, buddy. Just people problems. I'll make it up to you with some rabbit guts in the morning. How's that sound?"

The turtle just stared.

CHAPTER EIGHT

Before dusk could begin closing out the day, the first rumbles of thunder rolled across the horizon. The mountain was no stranger to storms at this time of year. A low grumble of sound, almost indiscernible from the wind, echoed around the rim of the ancient caldera, slowly growing in confidence. By nightfall, the wind was whipping the trees and the rain hammered down in torrents of liquid fury. At least the fire at the top of the mountain would be doused, eradicating its message. She wished she'd had the chance to ask Sarah about it. What danger it might represent. Was Darren calling others to the camp, or letting them know he was on his way? With luck they would move on tomorrow and normality – if you could call it that – would resume. There was comfort in routine, however hard life might be.

Cora watched the canopy from her perch, and worried. Most of the time, these storms blew through the valley and out of mind just as quickly as they blew in, but they could still do plenty of damage. A thin stream of water ran down towards the camp, one of many racing down the slopes, raising havoc on the way, loosening dirt and stones. During these deluges, her shack wouldn't cut it. Not against landslides. She'd shifted to a cave halfway up a steep hill above the gorge. She and Barney had been caught in a nasty storm when they first arrived and their first camp had been destroyed. This shelter wasn't ideal – the wind could cut right through it – but it hadn't failed her yet. It stayed mostly dry thanks to a primitive barricade she'd built from vines and thin woven branches across the entrance. Inside, there was room for a small fire in an old brazier she had found. She listened carefully. Thunder growled. Lightning flashed beyond the canopy and the wind whistled through the branches.

She wondered whether Sarah was still at the boat or if she had returned to the campsite. Cora couldn't see their tent from here. It was large and sturdy, but she doubted it was designed to withstand storms like this. The houseboat would offer them better protection. For some reason, she found herself hoping they'd found a good spot to ride out the storm.

The horizon flashed across the sky and another peal of thunder reverberated. Cora stoked the coals in the brazier and listened to the rain. It showed no sign of slowing. The rhythmic drumming of it, the fresh petrichor scent in the night air, along with the fierce warmth of the fire—such things would usually make for a great night of sleep. That wouldn't be happening tonight. She needed to keep watch just in case. She couldn't trust that Darren would be put off so easily. If Sarah revealed where she had hidden the gun, if he beat it out of her, things could quickly come to a head. The sky outside flashed again. The thunder followed moments later.

Something cracked outside. Squelched. It might have been the tread of a boot on a boggy mountain trail. Or something even worse. There, amidst the rustle of the wind and the beating of the rain, something scrambled. Slapped. Cora picked up a hefty length of stick and moved to the entrance of the shelter, peering out. She let her eyes adjust to the darkness. Thunder growled. A branch cracked. Something appeared in the foliage. A head-shape. Blurred by the thick wall of misty rain, it was hard to make out exactly, but the size and humanoid shape gave it away.

A big bastard lizard, drawn by the gunshot. It had to be.

There was a great rending sound as an old gum, rotten with termites, toppled with a terrific thud. Someone laughed then, from across the clearing. Brayed, almost.

Darren. Was he just ragging her, making her think there was a lizard out there?

The sky flashed, torn apart by light and sound. For just a moment, Cora saw him standing only metres away from the fallen eucalypt.

Something small burst out of the foliage and darted across the clearing. A wallaby? A possum?

Something else growled, beneath the thunder. Something bestial. As the rumbling peal dissipated, this animal noise continued, rising in intensity.

Cora didn't want to look away from the spot where Darren had been, but she had to move her head to triangulate the snarls. Because if it wasn't Darren making that sound, something else prowled the darkness out there.

She had to gamble. The hatchet hammer was in her bag at the back of the cave, but she also had a machete. And a broken hand-axe she used to cut lengths of timber. It could be risky, but there was no hope otherwise. Her knife wouldn't be enough. Not for a lizard. She slunk back into the shelter, pulling the makeshift screen across the entrance, and backed towards the brazier. The machete was closest. It felt good in her hand – a tool she'd come to know well.

Then came the footsteps. They came quickly and they came with purpose.

Something, or someone, fumbled with the screen. Cora thought about throwing the machete, but if her aim wasn't perfect, she'd be good as dead. She held it high, blade pointing shoulder-high.

The thing growled again. From the sound, it had to be farther back, beyond the fallen tree. Why hadn't it charged?

Darren slid open the barricade and entered the shelter with his hands up. Like his face, they were dry and cracked. She couldn't imagine how painful they must be. The skin was almost segmented. "Give me a weapon," he said.

Cora's pulse quickened. Her mouth went dry. In the confines of the hollow, she saw again – with stark clarity – just how big he was. She wasn't one to back down, but she realised there could only be one outcome if he decided to attack her.

Darren dragged the screen back fully to cover the entrance, wedged a prop against it. "Weapon! Now!"

The bushes outside exploded with movement. The screen shook violently.

His eyes met Cora's, and a flash of understanding swept across them.

Cora felt like the two of them had both had a premonition – a violent denouement – but this wasn't the time for it. She had to arm him. Now. "Axe!" She pointed to the pile of split logs.

A clawed hand burst through the screen. Already, the primitive obstacle creaked and cracked with the pressure. Vines looped like strings pulled against their knots; branches splintered. The fucking thing could be inside, ripping and tearing, at any moment. *That bloody gunshot!* Cora had never been trapped like this before.

The lizard's scabrous face smashed through the gap. One yellow eye was clearly visible, and its tongue flickered, perverse and lurid in the firelight.

Cora couldn't wait any longer. She slashed at the clawed hand still poking through. There was a thuck and a squamous finger fell to the ground. She side-stepped quickly as the screen shook horribly. The monster screamed and squirmed, but she was just as wary of the monster behind her. She'd have to keep him in her line of vision if she could.

Darren appeared beside Cora, hacking at the monstrous hands and face with the frenzy of a madman. The monster screamed again and the shaking stopped. It had let go. An ominous silence filled the cave.

Outside, the rain drummed on.

Darren didn't pay her any attention. He turned his back to her as he pushed against the screen. His shirt lifted, revealing the butt of the gun sticking out of his belt. She could only hope he hadn't found the shells. *Fuck.* She could kill him while he had his back turned. She had the weapon to do it; she wouldn't get a better chance. *Sure. And then, the lizard would kill her.* She couldn't fight them both. A growl from Darren signalled the start of round two, and the answer was obvious.

The monster hurtled into their barricade once more, head down, hoping to just barge its way through. The screen bent; buckled inwards. Darren stumbled back under the crashing weight of the impact. Bleeding and screaming, the monster tripped as it burst through, collapsing to the ground, its feet and tail whipping around for purchase. Before it could regain its feet, the two of them hacked into it savagely.

Machete and axe rained down on the beast. They were designed for timber and foliage but they destroyed flesh with equal ease. The thing squealed and bucked, flailed, and its arterial spray, when it came, gave an intoxicating catharsis. Cora pushed its head down with her foot and, between two ridged scutes above its spine, she found a fine lodgement for the pointed tip of the machete. She pushed, leaning on it with all her weight, until the blade sunk in. The creature's leg twitched as it died. Only then did Cora yank the blade free. Then Darren swung the axe down, over and over again until finally, he smashed the spine from the base of the skull and ripped the head free.

The same ominous silence that enveloped them prior to the thing's final charge swelled again. The rain beat ever on and the two of them, covered in blood, stood staring at each other. Cora held the machete tightly, knuckles white on the handle. The blade rested in the palm of her left hand.

Darren grunted and jammed the axe into his belt, calmly

flaunting his pistol.

Cora pretended not to notice and lowered her own weapon. "Where's Sarah?"

"Wouldn't you like to know?" Darren snatched up the lizard's head from the ground, strode over the broken screen and paused. "We're not done, you and me," he said, but he left. Cora let out a deep and shuddering breath as she watched him go. Dimly, she noticed that his spine seemed more prominent than it should. If he was starting to waste, the sickness ran deeper than she realised.

The pool of blood underneath the lizard spread out and seeped into the moist soil of the shelter. Cora grabbed the hideous thing by its legs and dragged it outside. She would take it down to the old campsite now, ready for burning in the morning. She needed it gone from this place. The rain would wash her clean while she did it, and what wasn't scoured away by the pelting torrent could be taken care of in the waterfall. It would surely be raging by now.

CHAPTER NINE

The sun blazed down. Aside from the clay-like stickiness of the mud underfoot, it was as if the torrential weather of the night before was just a dream. The birds sang once again, harking the arrival of another hot summer day, and the cicadas provided accompaniment. Neither of these sounds woke Cora, though. The flies did that. Despite her best efforts to scrape away the blood, the acrid scent of the lizardman's ichor lingered, and flies homed in on its location. They buzzed maddeningly around the source of the offending smell. The shelter would have to be abandoned for a while, at least until the stench disappeared. She could perhaps douse the area with water, but the rank smell of rot and decay would set in soon enough.

The sodden ground stuck to her feet like tar and squeezed between her toes as she went outside to stretch. The humidity was not yet unbearable, but it soon would be. It wouldn't take long for firewood to dry in this heat, and that was good. She didn't feel like carrying dry timber down to the old campsite where the dead lizard still needed to be burned. In a way, she should thank Darren for his help, but that was weighed against the fact the malevolent prick had brought the thing here in the first place with his gunshot. He had left the shelter in some state of truce, that was true, but the promise of future violence remained. She cursed herself for passing up a second opportunity to put the whole thing to bed. Morality was a luxury, she realised – the privilege of people who were safe.

She pondered this as she made the short journey down to the waterhole. She also thought long and hard about Darren—or rather, about what he might do next. The almost orgiastic violence that came with the monster's butchering seemed to have bled into a kind of one-upmanship that

Darren ended with the messy decapitation. As if that wasn't bad enough, Darren had taken the head with him, like a trophy. Whether this move was part of the pissing contest or indicative of something worse, Cora couldn't say, but it was deeply disturbing. If he knew what she had done, would this be her fate as well?

As she reached the end of the path, Cora stopped short. The severed head stared out, accusing, from the centre of her camp. Its left eye hung limp, while the right gazed balefully off into the distance. An army of flies buzzed, hovered, and landed to feast. The scaled flesh of the neck had clearly stretched and torn when Darren ripped it free from the rest of the creature. Thick blue veins and blackening tendons hung like the tendrils of some demonic octopus. A string of coagulated blood dangled and swayed from what had to be the major arterial passage, forming a crude stalactite. Behind it, a piece of spinal cord, the length of a finger, hung forlornly. The monster's jaw gaped, revealing rows of terrible predators' teeth, their days of ripping and tearing done. The tongue, swollen and purple, pressed against them and bulged through the gaps. The whole thing was skewered through the base of its gaping throat by a sharpened stick. This had itself been speared into the coals of the cooking fire near the water's edge, and was blackened where flames had licked along its length. Darren must have repeatedly beaten it down like a pile-driver to get it to stand upright like that. The lingering stench of flesh hung in the air, fly-blown and carbonised. Parts of the head had smouldered in the warmth of the still-hot coals. There were slits cut into the monster's cheek-bones, but these wounds were different to the others. They were not slashed in the heat of battle, but cut away in thin strips after the fact. It put her in mind of a ceremonial act. One of those strips lay curling at the base of the fire, half-chewed like old jerky. Finally, as she circled the thing, she discovered that its head had been scalped. The bare skull revealed below the tough flesh had been smashed like a coconut. And the brains were gone. Cora's stomach practically leapt behind her ribs in disgust.

She spun towards Darren and Sarah's tent. The front flaps were unzipped, swaying slightly in the low breeze. The tent hadn't fared too badly in the storm after all. Guy ropes had come loose and the canopy had shifted where loops of material had slipped from pegs, but it was relatively undamaged. She wrenched open the front flap. The tent was empty. Sarah's discarded clothes were strewn across the floor. Wherever Darren was, he had cleared out in a hurry and Sarah didn't appear to be with him. The craggy steep of the mountain loomed heavily above her and she had an idea where the bastard might be. He certainly hadn't been keen on the boat when the discussion was last broached. No, if anyone was there, it would be Sarah.

Cora walked back to the cooking fire, eyeing the grotesque gargoyle spiked above it, when her foot sent something spinning. It was only small, but the sight of it just about broke her: the scorched carapace of a river turtle, cracked open and blackened by soot. A small head lay to the side of it on the edge of the fire-pit. There was only one turtle of such size in this part of the creek. She didn't think this was a spiteful act – she'd never mentioned Maturin to either of her guests – but it stank of Darren's entitlement. He had food at the boat, but he'd rather eat hers. And in her absence? He just took what he could find. If the bastard had any actual idea of what he was doing, he would have made a bigger song and dance about it. Her pet would be mounted on its own stake beside the lizard. At this image, her nausea gave way to white hot rage. She'd hold on to that; it would serve her well later.

Holding the remains of her little friend in trembling hands, she choked back a tear. When she thought of how long she had been making friends with the little reptile, it was impossible not to think of Barney. He had fed it on many occasions, and was always enthralled by the gentle creature. The levee broke, and she decided she could manage at least one solid act of humanity today. She would give the little reptile a proper burial near her son. She took the turtle's remains beyond the balga plants and ferns up to the cairn where her boy lay, and dug a little grave.

When she was done, she went straight to the campsite where the headless lizard waited for its own ceremony. Flies droned heavily around it, the only creatures, it seemed, who could stomach its flesh. She thought then of the slices in its cheeks. Maybe not the only creature... A crow watched the proceedings from a low branch, cawing its commentary and pecking at the bark. She threw the disgusting corpse into the big fire-pit, built it up nice and hot, and then went to fetch the head. There was no way that thing was staying there.

As she returned, clumsy footfalls stumbled down the track from the waterhole. Cora rose to her haunches and pulled the hatchet hammer from her bag. It was likely that more than one monster would be drawn by the gunshot, but she hadn't expected to be interrupted so soon. She melted into the shade beneath the stretching limbs of a huge fig and waited for the creature to appear.

And then she gasped.

Sarah – bloodied and bruised – staggered into sight and collapsed.

CHAPTER TEN

Sarah couldn't say anything, but it seemed she'd been left for dead. All she could do was sleep. Hopefully she wouldn't lapse into a coma. There was nothing Cora could do if she was bleeding internally. The best she could think of to alleviate the bruising was to soak some rags in water and use them as a substitute for ice. She had made a proper fist of living wild, but there was no mistaking just how much had been lost since the world turned to shit. How much more simpler it would have been to call an ambulance just a few short years ago...

Much as she felt she should watch over Sarah, particularly with Darren still unaccounted for, she knew it was vital to get to the top of the mountain. The two of them had set a signal fire yesterday and that meant they were communicating with someone. Now Cora needed to know whether that someone was sending messages back.

The monstrous head burned merrily in the flames. Its eyes had boiled away; the tongue had burst in the heat; the once-green skin had crisped to blackness, and it all smelled noxious. Parts of it, particularly around the forehead, had peeled away, leaving the bone exposed. As she squatted, watching it smoulder, she noted the colour of the lizard's flesh, so similar to the necrotic sheen in the cracks of Darren's face. She thought back to what Sarah had said about their meat, the comments he'd made while the first lizard had burned, and the evidence of partial consumption here.

She'd heard the rumours about what could happen. After all, with so many displaced people seeking food and refuge in the early days of the chaos, the choice was simple. Find food or starve. Tales about how the meat changed a person were circulating in the early days, before

57

she fled the city. They seemed outlandish at best. Psychological stuff, for sure. Desperation brought out the worst of humanity, but a physical mutation? In the stories she'd heard, someone always put an end to the change before it could take full effect.

She couldn't help but see a reflection of her own struggles in all this. Here she was, isolated, yet desperate to hold onto everything that made her who she was. She knew the mountain was getting wilder. The days were hotter, the plants were growing more lush, and the storms, when they came, were fiercer than ever. She even knew in her heart of hearts that when fire eventually hit this place, it would be devastating, biblical, but she was desperate to hang on while she could. Her boy was here. She couldn't let go of him. And with him here, the mountain gave her a sense of place, of belonging. If she could conquer her territory with rules and order, she could hold on to her humanity.

She was burning a creature that hunted down and killed without mercy because that was what it did. It didn't have to think. It was a predator. Darren, on the other hand, was a man. He knew what he was doing when he beat the shit out of Sarah. Nothing could convince Cora it was poor anger management, bad parenting, or lack of a soul. It was pure malice, and that meant the real monster was the guy heading up to the summit. It had nothing to do with his physical appearance. Cora left the lizard burning, checked on Sarah, then returned to the wet-weather cave to grab some supplies. The mountain peak loomed, ever-present, above her and for the first time, she wished she had just taken the gun and shot the bastard.

When she reached the mountain's peak, the coals of Darren's previous fire were still cold and damp. He was nowhere to be seen, and it was clear the fire had been untouched since the rain had done its work. Below, the boat was still visible, but Cora could see no signs of life, even with her binoculars. Wherever Darren was, he was laying low.

Technically, there were two peaks to this mountain. The very top formed what could be referred to as a saddle. One peak, a hard spike of rhyolite, was referred to colloquially as the Finger, while the larger of the two peaks was known as the Eyrie.

A nearby bush rustled. A turkey came strutting out from underneath it, scampered across the track and into the bushes on the other side. She smiled at it. Of all the creatures on the mountain, turkeys were the ones that should have been the safest bet for eating. Cora had caught and cooked more than a few. Every single one of them had tasted like leather.

The cold remnants of the signal fire sat sombrely on the Eyrie in the midst of a ring of stones. There was a half-burned log about the length of an arm still lying prostrate in it. The small fire-scarred cubes of the blackened timber had carbonised, looking for all the world like a bite mark in a charcoal belly—and that drew her mind back to the partially consumed lizard. Why the fuck did Darren leave so much unanswered last night? It wasn't rational. She couldn't explain it, and she didn't know why it mattered, but there had to be something more going on here.

CHAPTER ELEVEN

When Cora returned to the swimming hole, Sarah was sitting on a rock dangling her feet in the cool water. Concentric circles rolled away from her ankles as she kicked slowly backwards and forwards. She looked up sheepishly when she heard Cora approach, letting her pensive expression linger before turning her attention back to the water.

"How you feeling?" Cora asked.

Sarah leaned down on the palm of her hand and shifted her weight.

"No, don't get up."

Sarah relaxed. "Probably about as good as I look. Physically, at least..."

Cora waited for her to say more, certain she was going to ask about the bullets, but she let the moment pass. "You hungry?"

"Nah." She grinned. An almost impish curling of the lips. "Got any more of those stale teabags, though? He's taken everything, the bastard."

Cora smiled and threw her backpack down to the stony ground. "He's gone, then? I wondered if he was on that boat of yours. Thought he might be up there." She pointed a thumb at the eyrie.

"Fucks me. We're supposed to have shot through and met up with some friends of his, but I don't like your chances."

Cora rinsed her water-boiling pot near to where Sarah sat. Guppies circled the woman's toes, nibbling at dead skin and slowly weaving in and out of her reflection. She filled the pot and took it to the cooking fire. "Things changed, then?"

"Yeah, things changed." Sarah flapped at a pestering fly. It buzzed out of harm's reach and looped around again attempting to land on her bruised face, only to jerk away from another lazy swipe. "I'd like to tell you he's gone for good, but I know him better." Her eyes were pained slits, but she took a moment to level them at Cora. "He thinks you've stolen from him, and he's not the kind of man who'll let that slide."

Cora sighed. "I got rid of them. He's too dangerous armed.

"Stupid. He thinks you've got 'em hidden away. He won't just take your word for it. He wants them back.

"And if that's not an option? I can't have him attracting more lizards."

"Run. He's done bad things. Always has; even before people had to. And if he has his way with you, it won't matter whether the lizards come or not."

Cora let the threat slide over her. Studied the waterhole. "Where do you think he is?"

"Maybe the boat. Maybe somewhere closer." She jerked her head towards the bushes as something rustled, fear flaring in her eyes, her breath seizing.

A goanna, nothing more, plodding through the undergrowth. "Are you still in danger?" Cora asked. "Looks like he left you for dead."

Gingerly, the woman touched a hand to her face – first, the swollen black eyes, then the puffy lips, and finally the cut on her cheekbone. "Nah. If he wanted me dead, I'd be dead. No thanks to you."

She deserved that. Cora tested the warmth of the water

with a fingertip. "Where's your cup? I'll have a delicious stale tea here for you any minute now."

She nodded towards the tent. "Give me a minute."

"I've got it." She was up off her haunches before Sarah could get her feet out of the cool stream. She disappeared into the tent, emerging a moment later with an aluminium cup in tow. When she had made the tea, she kicked off her shoes and dangled her own feet in the water, enjoying its refreshing briskness on her shins. Patterns of light swirled over her legs, rippling with the current. "You said you'd be dead if he wanted it that way, but I feel like I could say the same. We killed a lizard together last night. I thought he'd come for me, but when the lizard arrived, we fought it together. I thought he'd attack me after, but he just cleared out. Left the head impaled down here." She kept the next part to herself. *He''d eaten some of it. Its brains. The meat from its cheeks.*

"You're lucky. Maybe it was like an old army thing. Respect after a battle, you know? He's strange like that."

"He was in the army?"

"You couldn't tell? The guy's as military as they come. Doesn't shut up about it when he drinks. Won't tell you he was kicked out, though. Some sort of misconduct when he was at war."

"Great, so he knows how to get around the forest too. I don't even have that advantage."

Sarah swirled the cup. "If I was you, I'd be leaving this place and not coming back. Not for a good while anyway."

Leaving was a concept Cora had entertained from time to time, when the loneliness bit. Putting the forest and the mountain behind; trying to find a band of survivors, a community, but she knew it would never happen. Barney was here. Always would be. "I like it here," she said eventually. "There are worse places to die." She observed the colours of the forest: the lush dark greens of the lichens, the lighter shadings of the leaves and grasses, the greys of the boulders and escarpments; she listened to the gurgle of the stream and rush of the waterfall, the calls of a thousand different birds and the musical cadences of the cicadas competing with the sweeping caress of the breeze on the canopy above; she even savoured the scents of the damp earth and the small cooking fire. "Tell me about the people you were supposed to join up with."

"I don't really know much about them. Apparently, they're old army friends of Darren's; some of them at least. One in particular, though: name of Black. I've never met him."

"Dangerous?"

Sarah raised an eyebrow.

"Okay, stupid question. Are they a direct threat?"

"Hard to say for sure, but Darren and Stanley – that's Black's first name – go way back. Whatever happened to Darren, happened to both of them. Darren said they got their marching orders at the same time."

"You never met him?"

"Nah. He's from further up north. Somehow Darren got wind that he was still about, trying to start a community or something. Who knows? That shit never ends well. But Darren wanted to make sure he had me with him, so he came and got me from...well, he came and got me. His purpose suited mine at the time and here we are. Ain't life a fucking joy?"

She ignored the fact Sarah had left an entire tale unstated, and returned to thoughts about the lizard-head and Darren's sickness; about where he was getting the meat. Sarah's reaction last time had ended the conversation abruptly, but she needed the confirmation. "He's eating them isn't he? Whenever he can."

Sarah didn't answer straight away.

"Is he?"

"I don't think so. Maybe. He had dried meat. He told me it was snake. Wouldn't let me have any."

"You've never eaten one?" In a way, she wanted Sarah to say she had. It would help end her fears that the meat was actually changing Darren somehow. Mutating him.

"No, I haven't."

"He definitely ate some last night. How long's he been doing it? Was that when he started to get sick?"

"Why would he need to? I told you it was easy to find cans of food everywhere."

Cora pinched the bridge of her nose. "You can tell me. He's not here." She rose to her full height.

Sarah kicked her feet in the water, sending little waves lapping at the shore. "I barely know you. I don't have to tell you anything."

The water dragon on the branch was gone. It had obviously slunk back into the water at some point. Typically, Maturin would have made himself visible by now. She turned her attention to the flowered spikes protruding from the balga trees up the path. "Okay, you're right. That's not really fair of me. Just tell me how you ended up here."

Sarah rolled her eyes. "Jeez. If you must know, we were trying to get to Black and his mates. They were supposedly out there killing lizards and 'trying to unite lost people'; all that stuff.

Sarah thought about her next words. "If it's any help, I don't reckon Black's actually looking for us. Darren's full of shit when it suits him, but what's certain is that Black's mob investigates signs of life. Knowing the kind of people Darren associated with, I doubt everyone's welcome, but if they think you're useful, you're offered the chance to join them."

"Like Genghis Khan. No need to guess what happens if they don't want you."

Sarah nodded. "I daresay you've hit the nail on the head. Best to get on your bike."

"That aside, Darren will stay around to get his 'vengeance', and you've only got Darren's word about Black. What about these other people you got into trouble with; you think they'll be looking for you?"

"There were three of them tracking us. Darren killed them all. They would have sent scouts to investigate when they realised those three weren't coming back, but realistically, they'd be starting their search again. The chances of them finding us are slim."

"Three of them? Shit."

"I told you. You need to get the fuck out of here."

"We'll see. How are his tracking skills?"

"He's no stranger to hunting."

"Of course he isn't. And I've got my work cut out for me hiding your tracks as well. I've seen you move through the bush. You've got the subtlety of a freight train." She came to an abrupt decision. "Get what you absolutely can't leave behind and let's make a move. I want to be well clear of here before dusk."

"Wait a minute; I never said I'm coming with you."

"Got anything better to do?"

Sarah raised her hands, lost for words.

"Relax, I'm not leaving this place for good. It's *my* home. But I'll be fucked if I'm just gonna sit around the campfire and pray he's gone for good. Now, are you coming or not?"

Sarah lifted her feet clear of the stream and shook off the excess water. "You think we should go for the boat. See if the coast's clear and nick off?"

"Too risky. I'll take you somewhere else for tonight. Let's play it safe." She slung her bag over her shoulder and headed for the trail.

CHAPTER TWELVE

Visible above a break in the canopy, a thin trail of smoke wafted upwards in a kinked pillar. From this vantage point, it reminded Cora of a snake stretching loosely to the clouds. It came from another mountain in the surrounding range, but it wasn't as thick and strong as one would expect from a signal fire, rather it was the kind of smoke that might drift up from small cooking flames. With the still air and humidity resting heavily, the breeze hadn't had the chance to push it around and dissipate it.

"That him, you reckon?" Sarah asked.

Cora shrugged and kept walking along the path. "In a while we're going to come to a creek. From there, we're going to walk through the water for a bit, then we'll come out, making sure we leave footprints as we walk to the next creek before coming back to the exact spot we hopped out from to start with."

Sarah flapped her hand, her mind on more urgent matters. The uncertainty was getting to her. "Where'd you hide the ammo? You need it."

Cora gave her a steely look. "That's out of the equation. I told you - it's gone"

"How?"

She shouldn't trust this woman. She may not mean to, but Sarah could betray her with a stray word, or be put under duress. "I threw it in the river."

She hated the lie. It revealed a cynical side she wasn't sure she liked, but she had to protect herself. Sarah had come this far with Darren; that meant his protection was worth all the shit he'd put her through - worth it to her, at least. Cora couldn't afford to trust her.

Sarah stopped. "Are you serious? This whole time I thought you'd hidden it away somewhere, just in case. I can't believe it. Everything that's happened, and you actually thought it was a good idea to throw your only bit of leverage into a fucking river?" She raised her arms in despair. "You're an idiot!"

Cora squinted. "Are you finished?"

"I'm not sure I am!" She jabbed her finger at Cora accusingly. "I took it away so no one would get harmed. I was scared shitless he'd get gun-happy again, so I took it off the board. Why did you have to stick your nose in? This would have blown over by now, we'd have fucked off already.

Cora shook her head, but she kept her tongue between her teeth. Let her blow off steam if she needed to.

"I watched him shoot three people in the head; right in the fucking head. He's a killer, and you've pissed him off royally. It doesn't matter if his gun works or not, he will come back here and flat-out murder you."

"You keep talking like he's some horror movie psychopath..."

"He's worse. He's a real person who was trained to kill for a living and he wants you dead. Back in the day, he knew how to differentiate between the enemy and everyday people. There are no rules, now. Survival is all that matters, and he's become more and more wild since it all went to shit." She prodded Cora in the chest. "And you? You just keep pushing him. He's been stewing on that. He thinks you've wronged him, and he just wants you dead. He told me as much. Why do you think he had me take him to where I buried the gun yesterday?"

"Okay. You've had your say. If he comes, he comes. We're taking precautions to avoid that, and once we figure out a proper plan of action, we'll go from there. But listen, Sarah. If he *has* been eating them, it's not only the fact everything's gone to shit that's making him change."

Sarah massaged her own temples. "I can't hear any more of that shit right now. Give it a fucking rest until we deal with what's important."

They walked in tense silence until the rhythm of rushing water began to beat from up ahead. This was a smaller section of the creek which had its origins in the mountain. Gigantic rocks and boulders littered the ground and rainwater filtered through them, down small lips and natural dams. Up ahead it picked up impetuous pace again, swelling and tumbling against the banks.

"From here we wade," Cora said.

Sarah started to unlace her sneakers. They had seen better days, but she didn't fancy trudging about in wet shoes for the rest of the day.

"No. Leave them on. Bullrout."

Sarah's face showed no recognition.

"Freshwater stonefish. They live in the cracks. If you tread on one it'll sting you on reflex. Hurts like a motherfucker."

Sarah screwed up her face. "How far is it?"

"About a kilometre. I want to double back, create a false trail just in case he's following."

"You know where you're going?"

She had gotten so used to not interacting with anyone in her time alone, she'd forgotten how annoying mundane questions could be. How did this woman think Cora had brought them this far if she didn't know where she was going? "There are some old derelict goldminers' huts from the turn of the century. We should be safe enough there."

"You mean to tell me there are ready-made huts and you're living in a fucking cubby house?"

"Huts is maybe a bit generous, and they're riddled with termites. Hardly the Ritz. Well, you'll see."

Sarah grunted.

Cora splashed into the creek, heading towards the centre of the stream. She used a long stick to poke and prod at the riverbed ahead of her. "Don't slip. Take it nice and slow. Best hold on to my bag as we go." She cast her attention to the skyline where the thin trail of smoke still gently floated upwards. It wasn't out of the realm of possibility that Darren had already discovered the huts. He could even be using one for his own refuge now.

Small fish darted away from their looming shadows. "If it looks like he's been there, we'll find somewhere else. There's plenty of time before dark."

Up ahead, the buttress roots of a large fig jutted into the water. Centuries of sediment had built up around them, forming a kind of miniature promontory. They made their way over to it and Cora stopped before moving onto the embankment. "Okay. Take your shoes off now. We're going to walk barefoot across the ground for about three-hundred metres. There's another tributary creek there that forks and leads back out towards the road upstream. We're going to make a show of getting into that creek. Once we've done that, we're going to put our shoes back on, and head up towards those large boulders. Then we'll rock-hop into the forest again. From there we'll head straight to the old huts." She watched Sarah nod, tipped her own head in return, and took her shoes off.

The muddy bed was soft and she picked up several leeches along the way. When Sarah complained, Cora hustled her onward. "We need quick, light footsteps here. We're going to walk back over them with our shoes on later —hopefully that will cover the tracks."

Eventually, they made it to the next creek and Cora yanked the leeches off, flicking them disdainfully into the lush foliage. She put her shoes on before going into the creek, and made Sarah do the same. Finally, after a laborious backwards walk, they made it back to the fig tree. She could only imagine how battered and bruised Sarah was feeling. In fairness to her, the girl might ask a lot of questions, but she was tough.

They were both exhausted by the time they reached the forest, but they'd made good time. Cora glanced back in the direction they'd come. The original smoke trail was still there, but now she saw a second trail of smoke. This one was thicker: a signal fire. Definitely.

Sarah had clearly seen it too. "Has that been there all day?"

"I don't know. Maybe." Perhaps this meant Darren had left them to their own devices. If so, that might change things. She led Sarah through the forest and over several foothills on the way to the old huts. They were dilapidated, mouldy and full of cobwebs she'd need to clear with the stick, but some shelter was better than none. They couldn't risk lighting a fire. She held a finger to her lips and motioned for Sarah to crouch down. "Wait here. I'll check it out."

There were no signs of Darren in any of the shacks. The reddened sky had begun to dim as the sun set. A large carpet snake slithered through the rafters of one and a dozen bats hung in another. Spiders and rats scurried around the broken floorboards, away from her steps, but no one else had disturbed the wrecks in quite some time.

She went back to Sarah who jerked bolt upright when Cora called her name softly. She had a sneaking suspicion the woman had been dozing off. "Come on. It's not much, but it'll be safe tonight."

CHAPTER THIRTEEN

The night was warm. The forest was alive with the sounds of nature: bats squabbled in the trees, mosquitoes whined, frogs croaked in damp hollows, and the cicadas continued their mindless song. They relied on the moon and the stars to see by, fearing a fire would bring Darren down upon them. That meant there was no smoke to keep away the bugs. Cora thought she had grown used to the constant bites of incessant mozzies, midges and sand-flies, but here, in this swampier location they went for her with rapacious hunger. She tried to distract herself, and Sarah, with a bit of bush-lore. Small marsupials rustled in the ground shrubs. Cora recognised rufous bettongs, antechinus, and bandicoots – describing their distinctive features to Sarah. All Sarah could identify were the glow-worms dotting the undersides of branches and earthen embankments, but at least she took an interest.

There had been no sign of pursuit, but Cora couldn't have slept. She would have just lain there, working through endless plans of escape, survival and defence, in a cycle of fruitless anxiety. Instead, she paced the area, watching and listening for any signs of trouble. There was no reason to think Darren was anywhere close by, but Cora couldn't shake the feeling he was out there, biding his time, waiting for his moment. In this black mood, she wondered again why she hadn't just taken the gun and shot him. Or driven the pair away at gunpoint. And now she was being hunted. The thought gnawed at her.

In school, she had completed an assignment on how Aboriginal Australians had trapped and hunted game without the aid of firearms or advanced hunting weapons. She'd often considered what it must have been like for the first people who'd lived in this place for centuries upon centuries before European invasion, living off such a harsh and unforgiving land. They were resourceful, and any notions of their being dismissed as primitive were not just laughable, but woefully ignorant. In the early days, she had truly thought she was going to die from starvation on a number of occasions, though she had the benefit of nearby properties, nets and fishing line for the creeks. Without them—it didn't bear thinking about. Could she start again elsewhere? Did she have what it took to be truly self-sufficient?

She had been potential prey for more than a few lizards, but she had never had to deal with a predator as intelligent or cunning as another person. Could she stick it out here? Find a way to defeat him? If Darren was set on killing her and Sarah's fears weren't driving her to misread the whole situation, Cora was pitted against a trained and truly deranged soldier.

The thing that bugged her the most, though, was that this forest, this mountain, was her home. And regardless of the reasons, she didn't want to leave it behind. She was rooted in here now. Up on one of the other mountains in this great range, several birch trees, thousands of years old, had watched as the huge volcano weathered down into the granite ridges, dramatic peaks and spectacular plugs that defined this an ancient caldera. She would be one of those trees. Unmoving, unbending until the end of days; she would die before she abandoned her home—and Barney.

Floorboards creaked in the cabin. Sarah was awake. "Cora?"

"Yeah, I'm here." She used a large rock as a makeshift seat and waited. "What's up?"

"Have you...killed anyone before?"

Cora wasn't sure how to answer that.

Sarah sighed. "I didn't think so." Do you think you can live with the aftermath?" She sat herself down on a fallen

76

tree. "He thought he could, but I don't know. He's different now."

Cora heard a possum growl its whirring mating call, and wondered where Sarah was going with this. "You know I might not have a choice, right?"

Sarah rolled her eyes. "It'll change you. That's what I'm saying."

Cora thought of Barney again. Of her failure. Of the loss she'd endured because of her own mistakes. "Every day. Every day, I've stared into the abyss and I've had to decide whether I'm going to keep fighting or just lay down and die. Do you really think I haven't changed already?"

Sarah snorted. "You've been on your own for a long time and it fucks me how that didn't send you nuts, but what you've faced...that's not the abyss. You found a way to keep yourself whole. You've held on to your humanity while the rest of the world fell apart. What Darren's done – that's what changes you. That's what makes you a monster. No rules, and no consequences. So much 'freedom', you can barely feel yourself falling."

Cora stirred, angry now. "You don't get to tell me I'm fine. You don't get to tell me I've not been broken down by all this...all this shit!"

"I'm sure you've gone hungry a few times, I'm sure you cried when you lost your son, but compared to most people, you got what you wanted. You've been left alone. You've been safe. Yeah, the lizardmen are a fucking pain in the arse, but they're nothing compared to the people. Look at the grief *we've* caused. Imagine that every single fucking day, from every single fucking person you meet. So yeah, you've lived wild, and you've lost big, but the trees and the animals won't make you savage; other people will. That's why you don't need to kill him. Just get the fuck away from here. Live by yourself—or shit, find a community of like-minded survivors if you can, but don't become like him. Don't let him do that to you."

Sarah fell silent, but before Cora could respond, she spoke again. "Fuck this place. Leave it. You can find somewhere better."

Cora pictured Barney's ravaged body as she shovelled soil onto it. The rocks she piled on top and around it to keep the animals from disturbing him. Her last image of him would always be marred by the grotesque mutilation he endured in death, but he would always be her darling little boy. If only she could remember him properly. Whenever she closed her eyes at night, she saw him broken and bleeding. Never whole. Cora shook her head. Snarled. "This is my home. I'm not giving it up, and I'm not leaving him behind."

Sarah snorted. "This man is a fucking barbarian. Sure, you had your moment with him there when you killed that lizard, but he'll have been watching you and learning your weaknesses – and trust me, you have a lot of weaknesses." She sighed. "He'll put your fucking head on a stake, and there's no telling what he'll do with the rest of you."

"It's not that simple, though, is it?" She slapped a mosquito on her leg. "The way you tell it, he'll follow me anyway."

"It's possible, but not if I give him a reason to go in the other direction."

Cora looked at her, startled. "What? You mean you'd go *back* to him?"

Sarah observed her fingernails. "Here's the thing: I get it how it looks right now. You haven't seen anyone in ages, then I come along with my asshole boyfriend. He beats the shit out of me, you help me get back on my feet, and now you're acting like you own me too."

Cora wondered for a moment if Sarah had gone insane. "You couldn't be more wrong."

"No one thinks it's happening, but it is. It might not be a sexual possession, but companionship's a need, Cora. It doesn't matter if it comes from a skewed sense of responsibility, fucking boredom or...some hero complex. Whatever." She put her hand on Cora's shoulder. "It comes down to the same thing. You want to keep me. But what you need to realise is that if I can get him away from you, I'm the one saving you. You can have your life back again. It's nice to think that someone can."

Cora removed Sarah's hand. All kind of words were bubbling up, fighting to get past the rocks in her throat. It was insane! After all he'd done to her? She knew what kind of animal he was!

Sarah stood up. "You're missing the point, anyway. I could go back to him or strike out on my own – split his attention – but if there's one thing that's gonna *guarantee* he comes after you, it's me choosing – and that's the key word, 'choosing' – to go with you."

"And if I stay?"

Sarah's laugh was corpse-dry. "You'll die. Trust me on this. I get that you want to stake your claim to this place and make some sort of last stand that proves you own it, but look around you; all you really have here are rocks, clean water and some caves. Whatever you had here is gone. It's broken. Just face it and run. That's what I'm going to do."

Cora scratched a swelling bite on her ankle. "So why'd you get caught up in this at all? Why not just move on with him like you wanted to."

"I had a teacher tell me once that everyone whinges about people doing dumb shit in movies, but what no one realises is that people do dumb shit in real life all the time. People accidentally burn their homes down, they get emotional, they fuck up." She rubbed the bruise on her face. "I knew he was gonna kill you. I've seen him kill before, yeah, but you don't deserve it. You're not a bad person. Watching him murder you would have been like watching him quit." She wiped a tear from her face. "When

I took that gun, I did dumb shit. I fucked up. I should have warned you to clear out and I should have walked away. From you and him, because now you've fucked up too, and if you die, that'll be my fault."

In the near distance, the chittering screech of the possum whirred again. This time, though, there was an answer. A growling exhortation grew into an explosion of sound and a pained squeal. Both women craned their heads round towards the creek. Cora unclipped her knife. The cicadas intensified their sound, and the bats burst out of the trees, desperate to escape the apex predator.

"Get in the fucking cabin." Cora said.

Sarah didn't argue. She waited for Cora to come in behind her then tried to press the ill-fitting door closed. "It won't shut!" she said.

Cora whipped a finger to her lip and eyeballed Sarah. She looked through a crack in the timbers. Another roar tore through the foliage. "I'm going to lure it. You need to stay behind this door until I call for help."

"What the fuck?" Sarah hissed. "Just let it pass."

"Lizards don't just pass. If we leave it around, it'll come down on us when we least expect it."

The angry cicadas swelled again, and another shrill scream pierced the forest. It was getting closer. That was certain.

"So what's the plan?"

"I lure it. Force it to come in through the door." She dropped her bag to her waist and drew out the hatchet hammer, wishing she had brought the machete down from the wet weather cave. "When it comes through, I'll take its fucking knee with this. When it hits the ground, we smash in its head." She looked around. "Use one of those stones near the fireplace to brain it."

Sarah paused. "You sure this will work?"

"No option, but it did last time."

She stepped out of the hut. "Hey! Over here!"

Another terrifying roar raised the hackles on her neck.

"What are you waiting for?"

She ducked inside the hut and crouched low, using the wall as a shield. "Slam the door. Get its attention."

Pounding footsteps came closer as something huge moved through the brush. Then, came a loud metallic snap, and the lizard screamed in agony. Certain she knew what the sound was, she looked at Sarah quizzically. "Can you see it?"

Sarah shook her head.

She peered through the gap in the timber and saw the beast rolling on the ground, dragging a jaw trap behind it. *What the fuck?*

The lizard, yowling in pain, edged towards them, dragging itself forward with its taloned hands and pushing with its good leg. Its tail whipped furiously. The teeth of the trap chewed into the flesh of its calf as it beat its snared leg on the ground, trying to dislodge the device.

Cora gripped the hatchet hammer, and gestured at Sarah's rock. "Now. Before Darren hears."

She ran across to the scrambling monster and slammed the hatchet side of the tool into the top of the thing's scabrous head. It came down between two scutes, lodging tight, and the creature rolled away, thrashing.

Sarah brought the boulder down on its face, breaking its jaw.

Cora yanked the hatchet free and slammed it down again, and again, taking the lizard through the nose. She pulled her knife from its unlatched sheath and cut the thing's throat. She wiped the blade on the leaves of a nearby tree and kicked the creature.

"Bloody Darren did us a favour," she said.

Sarah wiped her brow and looked up. "What?"

"This trap. It's one of mine, but it shouldn't be out here. He set it. For us."

"When?"

"How the fuck do I know? We could have missed it by pure chance, or he could have snuck up and set it while we were inside. Either way, if one of us had trodden on it, we'd be telling a different bloody story right now."

"I need to go to the boat, Cora. If it's free, we need to take it and we need to get the fuck out of here. If he's there, then we escape another way, at least until he believes we're gone and goes looking for Stanley. We can't win this fight."

She hated it, but deep down, Cora knew this was the only logical option. At the very least, taking the boat out into the depths of the river would provide them with respite and a sense of security they didn't have here. If he tried to attack them there, they would see him coming a mile away. But first, she had to see Barney and tell him she was only staying safe for a few nights. "Just let me grab some things. Let me..." she trailed off. Was she really contemplating this?

"You need to run."

"I know. I need to go back to the campsite first, though."

"You're going to get yourself killed."

She turned on Sarah. Grabbed her by the strap of her singlet, pulling her closer and hissing her response. "I need to go back there, and I need to see my boy before I go anywhere. Once I've done that, then we'll check the boat, and if he's not there, we'll go deep into the river where we can watch him as he comes; have him at our mercy."

Sarah wasn't at all flustered by the aggression in Cora's response. "Whatever you say," she said. "But you've got your priorities backwards. We need to take the boat and leave him behind."

"Not leave. Pick him off if he tries to reach us, and if he's as angry as you say, he will."

"So why bother with Barney?"

"Because if it goes pear-shaped, I'll die knowing I did the right thing."

Sarah turned towards the trail, shaking her head. "Lead the way."

Cora started walking. The sun was already rising.

CHAPTER FOURTEEN

By the time the harsh sun had risen to burn its way through the morning mist, the two women were approaching the waterhole. They ignored the forking path that led directly to it though, and continued on, past the next dogleg bend which lead to Barney's cairn. Cora's tree-shanty was only a short walk ahead and the wet weather cave was a little farther.

"We're wasting time here. He could be tracking us even now."

Cora didn't take her eyes off the path. "Just keep an eye out for footprints or unusual patches on the ground. There was more than one trap in storage."

As Cora pushed up the run of a dozen stair-like sods – held in place by roots protruding from a particularly large tree – something heavy rustled in the bushes to their left.

"Did you hear that?"

"Sounded fucking huge. You got bloody yowies around here?"

"Probably a wallaby."

She walked towards the copse of bushes, the thick branch she used as a walking stick brandished in front of her. The rustling sounds halted.

"You think it's him?" Sarah whispered.

Cora paused at the edge of the greenery, her heart jolting as she pictured the big man exploding out of it; a perfect ambush. But no. That didn't feel right. There was something mindless about this; ignorant of humanity. She pushed the closest bushel of vegetation aside with the stick, and the whole copse shook. "Hello!" She stomped her feet, trying to get whatever was in there to show its face. The rustling stilled. She hit another branch with the stick and at that, the copse came to life. Dozens of creatures as tall as her knees burst out at all angles in darting leaps. She screamed, scrambling backwards, tripping on a rock and landing on her arse. Fucking wallabies! She looked at Sarah and laughed hard. The woman had all-but collapsed herself and was now clutching her ribs. "At least I know where to put my traps, now!"

Once they'd finally caught their breaths again, they climbed to the hut above the waterhole and looked out. The heat bore down on them like gravity and even the bugs cracked and popped beneath its pressure. From this vantage point at the top of a rocky foothill, the lower reaches of the forest stretched out beneath them.

"Look," Sarah said, aghast.

There were small fires like the one they had noticed last night, but scattered across the forest. Cora was grateful the wind hadn't caught them. With temperatures this high, it would take only one stray ember and a good breeze to set the whole thing ablaze. She wondered for a moment if that was what Darren was *trying* to do, and felt panic rise in her chest. If the flames took to the forest, there would be no hope for them; they were too far inside the verdant embrace of the old national park to make it out in time.

"Do you think he lit them all?" Cora asked.

Sarah shielded her eyes from the sun. "Without a doubt." She considered them carefully. Only relatively thin trails of smoke ghosted up into the air. "The bastard wants to leave us guessing. He wants us to know he could be anywhere."

The panic surged in Cora's chest again. Darren's plan was psychological. Worse, it was working.

"Come on," Sarah said, thumbing at the shelter. "Grab

your shit and let's move."

Cora scrambled in the dirt at the foot of her camping cot. She lifted a small plywood screen and pulled her small box of treasures out of a hidey-hole. The lock of Barney's hair, his baby teeth, and her old engagement ring were all still inside.

Sarah grunted in disgust. "You risked getting caught for that?"

"Don't even start."

Sarah raised her hands apologetically and stepped aside as Cora moved past her.

"We good to go?"

"Soon." She gestured for Sarah to follow, then headed up towards the cave above the gorge. As she turned to make sure Sarah was following, she saw evidence that Darren had been down to the waterhole. He'd left them a little gift, floating face up: a kangaroo. Mutilated. Blood pooled around it, contaminating her drinking water. From this vantage-point, the sickening swarm of flies buzzing around it seemed like an undulating black cloud, thick and bilious.

The creature had been sliced from arsehole to throat and its intestines had been pulled out and chopped so they could be used to spell one simple word on the dusty ground by her fire: DIE. It was written to be read from this angle. Her stomach flipped at the implication. She entered the cave with care, ready for anything.

The machete was gone. Across the rock-wall, written in great gobs of congealing blood, were the brutal words 'YOU'RE FUCKING DEAD', but even that abomination paled in comparison to the grinning face he'd drawn next to it. His fingers had trailed around rotated handprints, designed to smudge two blob-like eyes into the childish visage. They had the effect of gory eyelashes, and the trail of rivulets that ran down as the blood dried only added to the degenerate madness. Sarah heaved at the sight of it, but no vomit emerged.

With a shudder, Cora realised the bastard was only getting started. Before her knees could buckle, she ran down to Barney's cairn. Her own survival seemed a secondary consideration. Concern for Sarah disappeared as Cora pounded her boots on the dry and dusty ground. Low-hanging branches became a blur and the sounds of the forest diminished beneath the beating of her own panicked heart.

The leering face, the kind of thing she used to see in movies, existed in its own state of grotesque comical madness, but trapped in her thoughts, it followed her as she sprinted past the balga plants and their tall spikes, to where a length of liana vine plunged over a low-hanging gum branch above the cairn, swinging and creaking under its load. Cicadas whirred and buzzed while kookaburras, whipbirds and crows cast their coarse voices across the clearing. Beneath them, the smell of freshly turned earth and dry decay loitered in the air. Barney dangled from a noose looped into the vine, his skin dry and torn. The clothes she'd buried him in were tattered and stained from the chemical process of decomposition. The soft tissues were gone. Only a few remaining tufts of hair sprouted from his pate. Beetles and other insects alighted and crawled across his skeletal face. One of his shoes fell to the ground with a soft plop. And Cora staggered, fell to her knees. The air in her lungs was just gone. She couldn't draw breath. Her heart jack-knifed painfully, snapping out of its usual rhythm. She scrambled towards her desecrated son, misty with tears, a scream of rage and despair welling in her throat, when a blur of movement erupted from the bushes.

From the size and speed, Cora could have sworn it was a lizard tearing towards her boy, but where was its tail? It was only as she realised the powerful runner was Darren – shockingly bestial in posture – that she noticed the machete in his hand, arcing through the air at her child's throat.

She screamed, throwing her hands behind her head, pulling her knotted hair tight, but the blade continued its powerful stroke. Her son's legs kicked to the right as his head moved to the left. There was a horrible moment where he appeared weightless, then his body hit the ground, shattering into fragments. Knuckles bounced off the hard stones of his cairn and a shinbone spun into the bushes. His pelvis, still caught in his tiny cargoes landed on top of his fallen shoe. She howled denial, as the monster laughed.

Darren turned and reached out a hand to steady the madly spinning skull. Somehow, it hadn't fallen yet, and Cora thought for a second that at least that most sacred part of him was still fine. Then Darren yanked the liana out, splitting the skull at cheek and jaw, where it had been tied.

"Welcome, ladies. I thought you'd never make it!" he said, and tossed the remains of Barney's skull at her feet.

Adrenaline burned through her system as horror transformed into apocalyptic rage. She screamed and pulled the hatchet hammer from her bag.

Darren hurled himself at her in a flat run, tackling her before she could bring the weapon to bear.

She didn't know what hurt more, the sudden impact of his shoulder and forearm across her midsection or the bone-jarring thud when her head struck the ground. Barney's skull bounced and skittered away, dragging her desperate gaze with it. The big man's weight pressed down on her. "I'm gonna enjoy this you thieving little bitch." His voice was only dim, distant, until he forced her head round to look at him.

He leered down at her; predatory and animalistic. "You're lucky you took those bullets," he hissed. His face was blistered and peeling. Through her terror she couldn't help noting all the little details that marked him out as less than human now. His head was swollen, his skin had become ill-fitting. He closed his fist, and cannoned it into her jaw. She couldn't comprehend how her skull withstood the blow – how her brain wasn't spattered across the ground with her son's remains. She just lay there, stunned. Feebly, she tried to roll, to throw the man off her. He raised himself up a fraction, enjoying the squirm as she turned over. Blood ran freely from her nose and lip, splashing in the dust.

"Where's my ammo? What have you done with it?"

She raised an ineffective fist, as though to hit back at him, but he grasped it casually in his meaty hand and pushed it down. Darren's free hand wound its way into her hair, tight to the skull. He pressed her face down, forcing her to chew dirt. "Where are my bullets, bitch?"

The only response she could muster was a wail of helpless grief.

He lifted her face, yanked back her arm and twisted. "Don't want to answer?" He slammed her head down again, into the dirt.

Her vision shook. As though from a vast distance, she could hear Sarah screaming. Darren might have said something then, something about shutting the fuck up, but it could have been to either of them. Her head was yanked back again and she heard a sharp crack. Her neck; she was sure of it. Perhaps Darren had taken pity at last. She would be with her boy at any moment. He'd be waiting for her...

The weight shifted above her and his grip faltered. Softened and released.

"Get up. Cora, get up!" Sarah pulled at her. "We have to go. Now!"

She struggled to her feet, and shook her head, trying to clear the ringing in her ears, the blear from her vision. Darren lay sprawled; unconscious. *Dead?* A rock the size of a grapefruit lay on the ground beside him. "Did you—?"

"Bet your fucking life I did. Listen – do you hear that?" She pointed out into the bush, the distant sound of motorbikes echoing around. "Time's up. We have to get out of here."

Cora was coming back to her senses. Adrenaline had her synapses firing like pistols. Tears left streaks on her dirty face and she gestured to Barney's skull, upside down in the dirt. Pieces of him were strewn across the clearing. "You saw what he did." She drew her knife from its sheath. "That was my boy."

She centred the pig-sticker above his heart. There was no resistance in his head, no sign he was waking up. If she could end this once and for all, she could send Sarah on her way. It didn't matter that Black was coming. She'd be prepared this time; she could slink away into the depths of the forest until they passed. Things could go back to normal.

Arms tensed, muscles trembling, she raised the knife above her head and, certain Sarah would try to stop her, thrust down with all her might.

The blade plunged down like a fang, biting through muscle and bone until it thunked to a juddering stop, caught in a rib.

Sarah screamed, but Cora slammed the knife down, again and again, desperate to smash through the barrier. Ichor oozed from the wound, splashing out with the knife as she brought it back for the third and fourth blows, spattering Cora's rage-pale face.

Darren twitched and shook at this assault. Coughed blood. His eyes opened and he drank in Cora's hatred. He couldn't manage a smile, but she saw approval in his revolting yellowed eyes. She hammered the blade down again, savouring the hideous gasp. His tongue strained out with the foul breath – held...held – and subsided.

"Can't you hear that? Can't you fucking hear that?" Sarah tugged Cora's arm.

The motorcycles still droned on, the sounds carried on

the breeze from somewhere within the range. Cora couldn't bring herself to care. Bits of Barney adorned the ground all about her; scattered and shattered. She slammed the knife down one last time, and something cracked inside.

Sarah tugged at her arm, hysterical, and yanked her away.

Cora wiped the knife on his pants, eventually turning to face the direction the motorbikes were coming from. "Is he dead?"

Sarah felt for a pulse below his jawline. Nodded.

Cora turned back to her son's skull. "Good."

"Hide him in the bushes, but quickly; we need to move."

"You do it. I'll see to Barney!"

Sarah's face dropped. A darkness crawled across her face. "You don't have time," she said. "I'm sorry—but you don't."

Cora's lip began to quiver. "No," she said. "You're wrong." She wandered over to Barney's skull and cradled it for a moment. She gently kissed the exposed bone of his forehead. A thin layer of skin still stretched from the left side of his nose, across his eye and round the back of his cranium, but it wasn't him. There was nothing left to recognise. Her son was gone.

Sobbing, she grabbed what she could of the dead child's remains and pushed them back into the cairn, replacing the rocks Darren had dislodged.

She spat blood on the ground as she staggered back to Sarah, who was frantic by now.

"Get your head right," Sarah said. "We've got to hide Darren. They can't find him."

When Cora turned to track the vespiary of buzzing motorcycle engines, she noticed that far away on the other side of the vast caldera, a signal fire billowed portentous smoke up, up into the sky like a volcano boiling, ready to burst at the seams.

"Leave him," she said.

"What?"

Cora chewed a dirty fingernail, something she hadn't done for years. Not since her final exams in the days before. "You need to get to your boat and leave here before they find it."

Sarah looked at her dumbly.

"I'll stay here and rebuild. Rebury my son."

"You think they won't explore the area? That's what they do, Cora, they look for signs of life."

"You said Darren might have been bullshitting. Besides, with him dead, I'll be ready for them. I can hide deeper in the forest until they've cleared out. I'll take care of the body once we get you your bullets back. You might need them on your travels."

Sarah's face paled. "Are you telling me they're not underwater?"

Cora shrugged. "I lied. They're safe and dry. I just didn't know whether I could trust you. I thought..."

Sarah groaned. "Fuck it," she said. "It's not important. What if Darren was telling the truth? What if he and Stanley were best fucking mates and Stanley picks up where Darren left off. You won't be able to steal his ammo too."

Cora considered this. "It's a risk I can take," she said. I want my life to go back to normal." She thought of her son's defiled grave, the murder of Maturin, the violence that had taken place in her home. "As much as it can anyway."

"They'll find you."

As if to prove her point, the sound of motorcycles again soared across the sky.

"I've got warning this time. I can disappear before they come, but we need to move. Chat time's over." She retrieved the gun from Darren's body and wordlessly offered it to Sarah. "Take it," she said. "We're running out of time."

Sarah dismissed the gesture. "Put it in your bag. It's useless anyhow."

CHAPTER FIFTEEN

Cora held on to her knife like a drowning man with a lifeline. Her cheek hurt like hell and tears welled in her eyes. Darren might be dead, but they were out of time. They had to act now. Her feet slipped and skidded as she dove through the bush, trying to gather her thoughts.

The fucker had desecrated Barney's grave, and in doing so, he'd revealed death's raw truth. If she thought the boy had looked bad when she buried him, she was mistaken. Several months beneath the cairn left a bare semblance of the cherub she had known, and if she didn't get her shit together before Black found them, she may well end up the same way. Dying wouldn't have seemed so bad in those first few months after the loss of her child, when life's struggles felt so meaningless, but she never walked the path into the darkness. She didn't know what lurked within its cold valley, and there was no guarantee her son would be there waiting for her. She had never been a believer, not in the God stuff. She'd envied the certainty it brought some people, but she couldn't bring herself to swallow the fanciful stories. Perhaps that was why she couldn't give this place up. She needed to be here because Barney was here. All that would ever be left of him. Leaving now would truly be saying goodbye.

Sarah's houseboat was a problem – a flagrant sign of human life on the mountain. She needed to get rid of it, and she needed the gun – and its ammunition – gone too.

The luscious forest canopy closed in above them, and they stopped in the shade for a rest. As the wasplike sound of the motorcycle engines appeared again, the quiet chirping of a thousand different finches sounded from all around. Cora cuffed her snot and tears before finally sheathing her knife. "Sorry," she said, when they got their breath back. "I need to keep it together."

Sarah grunted. "You're doing all right. What he did... That would have destroyed me."

The incident had played over and over in her mind, but she could never see a way to stop him. She was done. Exhausted. Ready to drop. It didn't matter that Darren was dead. It didn't matter that she had won; the victory was Pyrrhic. He had damaged her in ways no one should ever have to endure. Even after death, she'd failed her son. In the days and weeks ahead, she'd need to come to terms with all of this. Figure out a way to go on in the wreckage of her life.

"You're sure this is what you want?"

Cora nodded, and stood up.

"And you'll be all right?"

She grunted and rooted through her gear, making sure her precious box was still safe. She really didn't want to talk about this. Regardless of what had happened, they had to be pragmatic. The world wasn't going to wait for her to get her shit together. The fact Darren was gone would mean fuck-all if Black or some other threat was just going to take his place.

Their next rest stop was in a clearing near the river. Cora stood stock-still and looked up at the smoke that plumed in the sky ahead. So much closer. "You think that smoke in the distance was meant to alert Darren that Black was on his way?"

"Undoubtedly. He was responding to Darren's signals."

The path forked and Cora turned left. Unseen beyond the tight canopy, the mountain's craggy steeps and sheer cliffs were high above them now, and this path, more of a goat-track, was sheltered from the worst of the sun. "You think he'll come in here?"

"We have to expect so."

"You're certain he's dangerous?"

Sarah rolled her eyes.

"That's a yes, then."

"To tell you the truth, I know fuck-all about him. Only what I told you before. But if Darren's whole plan was to link up with him, I can't see him playing nice. He was a cowboy, but he was always a cunning prick when he needed to be."

The whine of mosquitoes became noticeable and the swampy smell of stagnant water grew. Butterflies cavorted across their path. Cora shook her head. "We'd better move, then."

"I still think you're better off coming with me. Stay here and you might be dead by—" A metallic creak and blur of movement sprung up from below Sarah's foot, and she collapsed, screaming. The jaw trap bit through her shin and calf, its teeth clenched in an awful victorious grin.

Cora swiftly threw herself down to free her, wincing with empathy as she pried the teeth apart. Deep gashes in Sarah's leg ran with blood, soaking her sock and her boot. She clenched her teeth and pounded the floor with the heel of her hand, groaning and sobbing in pain. Cora rifled through her bag, certain she still had a bandage in there. "Can you move your ankle?" she asked, all business.

Sarah flexed her foot, gasping and choking. "I don't think it's broken," she said, through gritted teeth.

Cora didn't think it would matter whether it was broken or not. It needed stitches and antiseptic at the least. Shit, it needed a hospital. This was going to slow Sarah down massively. She wrapped the bandage around the wound and tried to ignore the flies which kept alighting on the seeping red patch.

"Help me up," Sarah said. "We've got to keep going."

"Just wait a minute. I have an idea." Cora moved the trap a few metres up the path and reset it. She covered it then with some deadfall and backed away. It was holding. Good. She helped Sarah to her feet, who gingerly pressed her weight onto her wounded leg and immediately collapsed again.

"Don't leave me here!"

"I'm not going to leave you, but you're going to have to hold onto me, okay?" She helped Sarah up again, then slowly, with Sarah hobbling along beside her, she led the way to the black pool beneath the fig tree. On top of the brackish water was a layer of detritus and leaf-litter washed in by the storm. Mosquitoes whined in the air above it. Revelling in the scent of sweat and blood, they took flight and homed in on the women.

Sarah slapped a mosquito. It exploded in a sanguine smear and she wiped the blood on her shirt. "What are we doing here? Let's move. These mozzies are the size of buffalo."

The hollow was just as Cora had left it. There was no sign it had been disturbed, but she still felt a surge of relief when her fingers brushed the first of the bullets. She collected them up and passed them to Sarah. "How many?" She watched Sarah's eyes narrow, certain she was considering the fact the bullets had been safe in this hollow the whole time.

"I'll count." If she was fuming inside, she hid it well. "Hurry up. I swear I heard someone."

Cora began rummaging in the hollow again as Sarah counted. No. She had them all. "You sure you heard footsteps?"

"Hard to tell with all the noise. Could be birds, animals, anything." She dropped the shells in her bag and surveyed the trees around them. The canopy was alive with the fluttering movement of birds.

"I think if they were here, we'd know."

Far above them, from somewhere in the vicinity of Barney's defiled grave, a primal scream ripped into the sky, drowning out the distant hum of motorcycles. It carried far across the forest, full of pain and rage. As it petered out, it broke into what sounded like a gurgling cough.

Sarah's eyes widened. "Lizard?" she asked, doubtfully.

"You know as well as I do what that was. I thought you said he was dead!"

"He had no fucking pulse! What am I? The fucking coroner?"

"Get to the boat," Cora said. "Now!"

No human could have survived that assault. Didn't matter how big he was, Darren couldn't be anything but dead or dying. Except he'd been eating that fucking lizard meat... and it seemed that the stories were true. He wasn't just sick; he'd been changing. Hadn't she seen the way his skin had altered? That raised spine wasn't his flesh wasting away—it was his fucking scutes growing. If that was him on the loose again, there was no way she could wait out Black and his men. There were too many enemies. "It looks like the plans have changed again."

CHAPTER SIXTEEN

By the time they had made it through the forest and out to the river, a hot wind had begun to blow. The trees rustled impatiently. Cora knew just how they felt. She just wanted to be gone now. Away from the feral madness that had shattered the remains of her life.

Cora surveyed the area. Her kayak, still tied to a stump on the embankment, was some way ahead. The houseboat, a boxy and forlorn shape, rested not far beyond that. They clearly hadn't been picky when they stole it. Like everything else these days, it needed a paint job.

The river shifted and stirred restlessly. Even at this stage of the afternoon, the moon could be seen high in the sky. "We can't take any chances. The kayak has to come on board with us."

Sarah grunted her assent.

Cora supposed that was good, but it wasn't as if she was giving her a choice. "You have keys?"

The wounded woman was pale. She had lost a lot of blood, and between the uneven trail, the constant assault by low-hanging branches, and the stress of their situation, it was all taking its toll. She patted her pocket though, and nodded, determined to make it to the boat.

A gust of wind whipped grit against her legs, the trees on the edge of the forest swished and swayed, and Cora had the sudden feeling she was being watched. "You think he's made it down yet?"

The pillar of signal-smoke from Black's campsite climbed into the sky like a great stairway, but Cora's gaze stayed low, surveying the shoreline. Darren had played a waiting game so far, but she had a feeling that shit may have changed. If the bestial roar they'd heard had been anything to go by, he'd probably come rampaging through the forest like one of the lizardmen, ready to tear them both apart. "I'd say he's closer than those bikes." Sound could travel for miles in the caldera, and while there was no doubt they were on the way, she was certain they still had time before Black arrived. "We need to stick to the tree-line – preferably a few metres in – until we're closer to the kayak. The less visible we are, the better."

Sarah nodded, her pale lips pursed with worry, and they slunk back under the trees. Dead leaves scurried across their path in the warm breeze, and the canopy shook, causing the crows to flap and caw. A fat drop of sweat tumbled from Cora's brow, but she hurried her pace, intent on her goal. Sarah trailed behind. When the kayak was within a stone's throw, Cora ducked down and peered out. Sarah caught up after a minute or two. "I'll need to check it before we go up. Rest here." She handed Sarah the gun and ammo. "Take these. I can't use them while dragging the kayak anyway. You know what to do.'"

Sarah winced. Nodded. She was weak. Deathly white.

Cora wasn't sure the girl would make it through the night. Sarah was tough, but that fucking trap had done too much damage. She pointed at an overgrown copse in the near distance. "If I was him, and I'd spotted us heading this way, I'd be waiting in amongst that lot. Well hidden. Good view. Once I've made sure it's clear, I'll come back for you."

She ran for the kayak, watching other concealed spots for sign of Darren. She flipped the vessel and dragged it across the rocky sand towards the houseboat. The scent of smoke blew past her nose again, and with it something else. A rank, animal smell. She turned slowly, watching for movement, but there was nothing out of the ordinary. *Fuck. Was he on the houseboat?*

Cora stopped in her tracks, frozen by indecision. She

turned to look back towards Sarah. Her heartbeat quickened and the hairs on her neck stood on end. Wind rushed in the hissing canopy. Sarah was thrust out of her hiding place with a cry of dismay, and pitched headlong into the sand.

Darren stepped out from behind her, grinning like a particularly smug gargoyle. Cora could scarcely comprehend his transformation. She could never have pictured it going so far. The front of his shirt was a ragged mess, stained with blood, but the physical changes had been sufficient to bring him back from the brink of death – a revenant of rage and retribution. He was here to complete her destruction. The peeling patches on his face were worse now. It was all necrotic, infected and green, oozing with pus. The swelling blisters were now protrusions and his mouth appeared to be cracked and bleeding at the corners. The fissures stretched right the way back to his ears and his eyes – it was hard to tell at this distance, but they seemed to be a lurid golden colour. Lizard eyes.

She grabbed the paddle and abandoned the kayak, leaving it rocking from side to side on the embankment and leapt towards him.

Darren's smug grin ripped and shifted into a rictus of joy. His torn lips gave it an extra degree of insanity. His teeth were huge. He kicked Sarah in the guts. Once. Twice. Brutal and sharp. "Come and get her."

Sarah writhed at his feet, coughing and gasping.

A trail of bleeding saliva dripped from the corner of his mouth like venom as he grinned at Cora. His eyes might have changed, but that cynical spark of intelligence still loitered behind them. As she approached, she saw that his skin was more than just irritated; it was coming apart at the seams, sloughing like a snake's. The verdant bruises beneath his eyes were corpulent with infection. Contusions marked his neck.

"Come on!" He jutted his head forward like a lizard

fronting up to a threat. With bloody teeth bared, he made a fearsome sight. Sarah crawled to the side, helped along by a saurian kick.

Cora flicked her rucksack off her shoulders and tossed it Sarah's way, then she brandished the paddle as a makeshift spear and made her approach. The wicked wind raced, scattering loose branches and detritus. She jabbed the paddle forward and tried to catch Darren in the balls, but the big man was ready for her.

He grabbed the shaft and pulled it into his body, trying to yank it out of her hands.

Vastly overpowered, Cora used the momentum he gave her and ran forward, thrusting the weapon at him, catching him in the belly. Feeling his grasp loosen, Cora yanked it back and swung. It whickered as it sped through the air.

Darren swiped at it with his arm, attempting a clumsy block and the weapon juddered against his elbow. He roared in pain, then put his shoulder down and charged her.

Her breath exploded from her with the impact. She hit the ground and saw Sarah fumbling with the gun, a look of panicked determination on her face. Desperate not to feel another of Darren's freight-train punches, Cora spun to the side.

Darren raised the oar like an axe, and swung it down, missing Cora's head by inches.

Sarah, done fumbling, levelled the gun at Darren, who roared with animal fury.

And *something* answered.

Cora saw it coming, sprinting towards them from the treeline.

Sarah levelled the gun as it leapt.

Everything melted into slow-motion.

The lizard flew through the air, talons extended, spittle dripping from its forked and madly lolling tongue.

Sarah pulled the trigger and the gun boomed. The lizard torpedoed towards Darren and its trajectory took it in front of the shot. Blood splashed from its shoulder and it barked its own throaty scream.

The monster struck Darren, latching on with its claws, knocking him to the ground and the two rolled into the bushes in a blur.

Cora grabbed the paddle and dragged Sarah towards the houseboat as the battle raged on in the bush. She snatched up the strap and dragged the kayak up the ramp.

Sarah started the engine and Cora secured the ramp, and the houseboat pulled away from the bank.

CHAPTER SEVENTEEN

The wind might have picked up, and the burning sun might have begun to wane, but the heat of the day still loitered in the houseboat's aluminium ceiling and stuffy interior. Cora steadied herself with one hand as the boat rocked. She could still hear the engines of the bikes and hoped that wherever they were, they couldn't hear the boat. "Head West."

"What about Black?" Sarah asked weakly.

"That's why we go inland. If we head towards the coast, we'll be going towards him."

"So you've made your mind up."

"What did we say earlier? Things change, right? Well... things changed."

The engine spluttered and Sarah tapped the fuel gauge. "Fuck!"

"What now?" Cora asked.

Sarah's head dropped, as if she was nodding off, then she sat back upright. She tapped a gauge.

"There's no fuel. He must have punctured the tank. There was loads when we got here."

"What? Why would he do that?"

"I feel like shit," Sarah said, staggering to the window. She dry-retched, but there was nothing much to bring up.

Cora caught her as she fell back, noting the small crimson pool beneath Sarah's stool. "Tell me there's a first-aid kit. Please..." She had to stitch Sarah's wound. She killed the engine then guided the wounded woman to the unmade bed at the end of the open-plan area.

"Anchor," she croaked, her eyes rolling back. "The remote's on the deck."

Cora found it, thumbed the switch, and looked up and down the riverbank. It couldn't be helped. She had to stitch the leg now or Sarah would bleed out.

The houseboat was obviously a rental set up for families. A small two-bed bunk was pressed against the side of the area. A couch, dining table and chairs took up the rest of the space beyond the small kitchenette. She raced to the cupboards lining the walls of the kitchenette, and started rooting through them. "First-aid kit?" she called.

"Down there." Sarah pointed at a trapdoor up towards the helm. "In storage. On the shelf."

Cora scrabbled around down there, in the dim, cramped orlop until she located the first-aid kit. It was yellowed with age, but it was a good size and had a reassuring heft. As she grabbed it, something knocked against the hull, right in front of her, with a dull thump. Once, twice, as if asking to come inside. Cora's heart picked up pace. *Nononononononono.* She scrambled up the ladder and dashed out on deck to see what had caused it. A branch, she saw with some relief, caught in the rippling current. It thudded against the houseboat again before spinning off.

The shore was a good hundred-and-fifty yards away, but her guts clenched at what she saw there: the lizard. Dead. Splayed out on the riverbank in a gruesome parody of nonchalance – propped up on one elbow, its foreclaw tucked under its chin as though it was sunbathing. How the fuck—? The wind was howling now across the open river, and her fear sang with it. He was still out there, then. *Christ.*

She felt the familiar weight in her chest settle and curl another icy tendril around her hopes of survival. Sarah groaned in pain, bringing her thoughts back to her first priority.

Sarah had moved to a chair by the starboard window, pressing the wound closed with both hands. "Hurry up." Cora began to unravel the sopping red bandage. Not only were the wounds deep and savage, but the flesh on either side had swollen; it was a vivid purple. A layer of dirt encrusted the congealing blood and sticky scabs. The wound might not already be infected, but given its severity and the conditions she had endured, it could only be a matter of time. *Okay. Suture kit – check. Fresh bandages – check. And, finally, antiseptic.* She doused her hands with the ancient bottle of hand sanitiser, rubbed them dry, then used Sarah's Zippo to sterilise the needle. Through the window, behind Sarah's head, Cora saw Darren emerge from a lush bank of ferns and lantana, his arms laden with wood. He squinted out at them and waved lazily.

Cora felt her breath catch but tried to concentrate on the job at hand. There was no point announcing she had never done this before; no point in trying to be gentle and professional. She needed to stop the flow of blood. Pretending she was stitching a hole in a pair of pants, she pushed the curved needle through a puffy lip of flesh that hung from the base of the wound on Sarah's shin, and quickly lanced it through the opposite flap, bridging the gored skin.

Sarah hissed.

Patient as a crocodile, Darren lit a campfire. A thin column of smoke drifted up into a sky that was beginning to show patches of purple as the sun lowered. Dusk was upon them.

Cora realised she hadn't heard the bikes for a while. Perhaps they'd decided to call it a night. To wait for the morning.

"He out there?" Sarah was watching Cora anxiously.

Cora nodded, sick to her stomach, then brought the

needle round for another loop.

The bastard rolled the lizard over now, confident his display had been seen, and he hacked a forearm off.

Cora saw her boy's dead face, staring out at her from the swinging vine as the monster's machete met his neck. She timed her stitches to the pendulum swing of the liana as Darren began to cook his meal.

"And Black?" Sarah asked.

"No sign. Yet." Cora closed off the final stitch needed to stop the shin pissing blood. She finished by pouring antiseptic on the wound. Sarah's clenched scream barely registered.

She moved to Sarah's calf next and repeated the process.

"This is going to kill me, you know?"

Cora knew, but she was doing the best that she could. What else was she going to do? Roll over and wait for the inevitable? *Fuck. That.* "Don't be a baby," she said. "You've survived worse."

Sarah wouldn't believe her, but that was irrelevant now. She needed her to have some spine. If Cora was going to stand a chance of winning, she needed this girl's help. Not to fight, but to split Darren's attention.

Sarah smiled. "You don't deserve all he's done. I'm sorry we came here. I'm sorry about a lot of things."

Cora grunted. What was she supposed to say? She glanced out of the window. The lizardman's arm had been left to char. Darren stood at the edge of the riverbank, and he was looking directly at her. As their eyes met, he drew the machete across his throat, symbolically, and tore his shirt off. Even from this distance, and in the weakening light, she could see that his torso was almost entirely green now, with blotches of cream on his belly.

"Sarah, look."

Before the wounded girl could even turn her head, Darren dove into the water.

CHAPTER EIGHTEEN

The sun had almost disappeared from sight, aside from a glowing radiance the colour of a bruise, melting behind the silhouetted ridgelines and slopes of the mountain. It wasn't enough. Any lapping wave could be Darren's rising form but Cora couldn't pick him out. A particularly loud splash had her jerking her head to the left, only for a heron to flap past the houseboat. From the shadowy tree-line on the riverbank, a curlew screamed its eerie childlike cry, as the boat rocked beneath the buffeting wind.

Sarah limped onto deck with a large torch in one hand and the gun in the other. She passed them to Cora wordlessly.

Darren's campfire glowed red, and as she swept the torch across the water, she had to stop herself from flinching at every reflected sparkle of light coming from beneath the surface.

Sarah leaned against the portside railing, holding herself steady with both hands. "Where the fuck could he have gone?"

Cora wanted to scream, but she bit it back, keeping her voice low and savage. "How should I know? One minute he was there and the next he was in the water."

"I don't see how he can hold his breath so long."

Why wouldn't she shut up? She was going to be useless in a fight; and her chatter was a distraction. "Just keep your eyes open."

Laughter rattled out of the darkness like gunfire from the opposite shore. Cora swung the torch in the direction it had come from. There was a splash and then only the familiar sounds of the forest could be heard. Squabbling bats. Cicadas. Curlews screaming like murder victims, and, of course, the rush of the wind.

A huge clang rang out and the hull shook somewhere near the portside bow. Cora ran around. The water was turbulent. A long, slow scraping sound ran along the underside of the boat.

Three more thumping clangs shook the vessel.

Then that scraping sound appeared again.

The women were becoming frantic now – Cora dashing from spot to spot, Sarah retreating to the cabin wall, a low wail building in her chest.

Another clang, this one on the starboard side.

Cora pointed the pistol over the edge and waited.

The boat jerked forward. The anchor winch rattled. Water sloshed.

Darren's laughter echoed out from below. There was a splash and the boat rocked. No sign of his body, but a wake raced from the hull out into the water.

Cora fired the pistol at it, her nerve shaken.

His laughter resounded once more.

One of the boat's windows shattered and glass crashed to the ground next to Sarah. She shrieked.

A rock the size of her fist lay amongst glass shards.

"Where is he?"

"There!" Sarah pointed to a spot some hundred yards away from the boat, halfway between it and the shore.

"Where?"

"He's gone. I saw his head."

Cora held the gun out, sweeping it across the water, ready to shoot as soon as she saw him.

A huge splash came from the bow end of the boat.

Cora ran to check it, but Sarah stopped her.

"He went under," she said. "He's gone already." And then her eyes widened as she looked back to the stern.

Cora turned to see a huge hand, clawed and scabrous, flexing on a cleat near the stern.

She levelled the gun, knowing there was no way she could hit such a small target.

"Shoot! Fucking shoot!"

She pulled the trigger, certain that Black and his men would hear the explosion of sound. The shot missed. She swore, and steadied her breath. She just had to wait for a better target. As soon as he rose above the rail, she could blast him.

A blur of motion erupted out of the water. A reptilian head appeared for a split second as Darren looked onto the houseboat. Cora pulled the trigger three times. The bullets whizzed harmlessly into the distance and then he was gone again. The reports echoed off the mountain. She listened, trying to locate him. She heard motorbikes. *Fuck.*

Three loud knocks rang out from the hull.

He reappeared.

Her next shot missed as well. So did the next one. And the next.

This time, he didn't knock to announce his presence. He laughed. When he sprung up the third time, his clawed and squamous hand lashed out and as she fired twice more, a projectile flew from it. It smashed hard into Cora's stomach, knocking the wind from her.

She collapsed to her knees, dropping the gun. She scrambled for it, but she was too slow. It bounced towards the railing, bounced again, and came to rest on the precipice of the deck, ready to fall into the water.

Darren, now a huge and powerful creature, humanoid in shape and saurian in appearance roared as he raced towards it.

Cora scrambled for the weapon, knowing she had to reach it before he did.

He rounded on her, yanking her up by her hair, and cast her backwards against the cabin wall. The fibreboard cracked under the impact and she gasped in pain. His other hand whipped up, holding the machete. Her legs gave way beneath her as he plunged the machete at her, slamming it into the wall where her head had just been. She looked up at him, looming over her, and she had never felt so utterly overwhelmed. What did she think was going to happen here? His eyes, lurid gold in the dying light, narrowed beneath scaly growths on his brow. The swollen protrusions Cora had noticed earlier had broken the skin at last. Scutes, like those on a crocodile's back, had burst out of his face like molars pushing through gums. Worst of all, though, was his mouth. It had split at the corners entirely, and stretched back to his ears. There was nothing human about those features. His incisors were gone. So were his canines. In their place, stunted like baby teeth, were the beginnings of crocodilian fangs.

She kicked up at his balls, hoping to hit the sweet spot, but his crotch was solid now. Internalised.

He grinned.

Pounding footsteps thundered across the deck, and Sarah, screaming with the agony of her effort, smashed into the monstrous man. She thumped into his back, sending him sprawling into the rail. The gun lay at his feet, still only millimetres from falling into the water.

He roared with laughter, and snatched the firearm off the deck. He spun, and pulled the trigger.

The blast resounded, ringing in Cora's ears.

Sarah's face crumpled as smoke curled from the weapon's barrel and blood gushed from her mid-section. She fell.

Cora screamed and Darren turned the gun towards her. That cavernous black barrel loomed and she knew that her time had come.

His finger twitched.

The weapon clicked.

He fingered the trigger twice more, but nothing meaningful reported. He roared; threw the gun into the water and stepped forward.

She reached for the machete, still juddering in the wall. The palm of his left hand shot out and smashed her in the face, mashing her lip against her teeth.

As she clutched her mouth, he yanked the machete out of the wall and turned back to Sarah. Cora fought to shake off the pain. She wiped the tears from her eyes and unbuckled her own knife, paltry by comparison. She heaved herself up.

He held the blade out in front of him, his wrist twitching in anticipation. Sarah retreated, scrambling, dragging her wounded leg, painting the deck with her life's blood.

Cora grasped the pigsticker and tried to remain quiet as she willed herself to move towards him, her eyes probing for anything that looked like a chink in his scaly armour. Her heartbeat, a rampaging jackhammer, climbed another notch as the sound of a motorcycle cut through the night. She forced her shaking hand up above her head, ready to bring the knife down between his shoulder blades with all her might.

Sarah saw what she was about to do and screamed, "Now!" She leapt onto the machete blade, impaling herself as she grabbed Darren's head. She wrapped her hands around his cranium and bit into his nose, clenching down with everything she had.

Cora was appalled. She couldn't move. She stood there, dumbfounded, as Sarah kicked forwards off the railing, shoving Darren through the gaping cabin door.

The blade stuck out of her back like a rudder, dripping gore, while Darren's outraged howls drowned out everything else.

Cora, stunned into action, took her opportunity. She thrust her knife towards his eyeball, hoping to plunge it into his brain. He turned at the last second, and the blade bounced off his saurian brow.

He fell backwards as she hammered the blade down again, landing awkwardly on deck before the open trapdoor. Sarah landed on top of him with a hollow gasp, and he thrashed, thrusting her aside, losing his grip on the machete.

As Darren climbed to his knees, Cora snatched up the previously discarded paddle. With both hands on the handle, she sprinted forward and jabbed the blade into his throat, catching him off-balance. He toppled backwards, down the hole and into the orlop with a crash. Cora slammed the trapdoor shut.

She dragged the couch over it and piled as much as she could on top of that. Even then, she doubted it would hold him for long. Earlier, she had seen methylated spirits in the kitchen while she was looking for the first-aid kit. She ran for it now, sloshing it across the curtains, onto the deck, and all over the couch.

With Darren slamming the trapdoor from below, she rummaged in her bag for flint. And then she recalled one of Sarah's earliest gestures. The tough little bitch had a

Zippo. She grabbed it out of the dead woman's pocket, struck the flame and pressed it to the couch.

Darren pounded the trapdoor with his reptilian fist, but he was too late.

Cora kissed Sarah on the forehead, and whispered goodbye. The cabin, burning hot now, began to fill with the sound of Darren's screams. She tossed the kayak over the side and leapt after it with the paddle in tow.

CHAPTER NINETEEN

After dragging the kayak ashore, she dropped to her knees and watched as the blazing houseboat began to collapse in on itself. With the wind tearing across the river, the threat of the fire spreading was real and present. The red and orange glow illuminated the water and a pillar of Stygian smoke, dense and oily, poured out of the vessel. Buffeted by the wind, it stretched across the river, choking her and leaving soot on every tree-trunk. Cora lifted her shirt over her face and crawled upriver.

Jets of flame belched outwards, and a huge explosion sent a rippling heatwave rolling across the water. The kitchen gas-tank had ruptured. Birds and bats went ballistic, screaming and flying out from the trees in all directions.

Again, she heard the motorbikes. They were here now, and at times, she even thought she could glimpse the distant glow of headlamps coming from the east. Those flying embers changed everything. She would be mad to hide in the belly of the forest now. She was mentally steeling herself for a long paddle up-river, when she heard a thump and a creak of metal, out on the wallowing hulk. A black shape moved and dipped, silhouetted against the conflagration. It crawled out of the wreckage and dived into the river.

The feeling of relief dissipated and the despair she had felt for hours gripped her again. Its clammy hands were cold and unrelenting. She was fucked if she couldn't take the monster out of the equation. On water, Darren's threat was insurmountable. He could easily drag her from the kayak and drown her. On land, he would be nearly impossible to stop – just like any other lizard – but she had to do something to take his advantages away from him, and all she could think of, even with the threat of fire growing, was the murder hole.

She thought back to the events of a few days ago and the lizard she'd lured into her trap right before Darren and Sarah arrived. It wouldn't take long and there were no signs of flames on her side of the river yet. If the fire stayed away for even another ten or fifteen minutes, that'd do it. She took a deep breath, steadied herself, cupped her hands to her mouth, and whooped.

That done, she ran, knowing she had to lead him; had to stay far enough ahead to lure him, just as she had that other lizard. As she sprinted through the trees, she tried to concentrate on just how she could manage. She had to break the chase into sections, and she knew just where to lead him first.

Within moments, his pounding footfalls drummed behind her. He slapped every tree as he passed, calling insults as best as he could through his scaly lips. "I'm gonna gut you, girlie." "You'll burn in a ditch." "I'll piss on your son's bones." He was enjoying the chase, making sport of it—and that, she hoped, would be his undoing. Even in the short time she had known him, it was clear he was ruled by his rage and self-regard. Nothing else mattered. She had to make her run look as panic-stricken as possible. Had to make him think she was blind with terror; his for the taking. "You'll bleed, bitch."

A fork split the path ahead of her. As the first hints of bushfire smoke wafted past her, she veered left. The pool and the fig where she'd hidden the gun were ahead. She pushed forward. Her tangled wet hair slapped her neck and her bag bruised her back as the hatchet hammer bounced, but she daren't stop to reposition it. All of this was coming to an end. She would be with Barney again soon, one way or another.

A beetle, fat and black, crashed into her, its hard chitin shell stinging the soft flesh of her cheek. Fireflies loitered on the path, and again, that smell of smoke gusted past her. The leaves whooshed, but this time the susurrus was different. Maybe it was her imagination, but it sounded desperate; terrified of the fire that was now undoubtedly raging on the other side of the river. She hoped it hadn't already reached the foothills beneath the craggy steeps of the mountain's bulkhead, hadn't already sent snaking feelers out into this stretch of forest.

In the near distance, the boughs of the ancient fig stretched towards her like a mother's embrace. Cora ran towards the murky pool in the shade beneath it. She re-oriented, seeking Barney's cairn in the heights. *There.* Skirting the stagnant depths, she took a moment to glance behind her.

He was shockingly close, cutting a swathe through the forest, spitting vulgarities. He swung the machete – Cora's machete – at every low-hanging branch in his path, scattering leaves, twigs, seedpods; juggernauting towards her. His inhuman eyes blazed. Behind him, an ominous red glow rose above the canopy.

Cora raced on, driven by terror and hope. She barely spotted the trap, but she managed to adjust her footing at the last second, leaping over it. She had to draw him into it so she put on an extra spurt of speed. The jaws slammed shut around his ankle with a metal shriek and Darren howled in outrage, falling to the ground in a cacophony of clanks and curses. Cora slowed at this. Stopped. Could she finish him here? Even as she turned to face him, he was up again, limping forward, dragging the trap behind him. He snarled some obscenity, and lunged for her. She sidestepped, and backed up, pleased with her work. His words were so mangled now, they barely registered, but the tone was unmistakable. She skipped back another couple of steps, making him work for it. He could hardly run with that thing on his leg. He seemed to reach the same conclusion, squatting down to free himself. She debated whether to risk getting the hatchet hammer out of her bag, but he pried the jaws open with relative ease. *Too late.* He hurled it aside and licked the blood from his fingers. *Fuck. Fuckfuckfuckfuckfuck.* Her chances of beating him one on one were minimal, even with this injury. All she could do was try to wear him down first.

"Come and fucking get me." She burst into another sprint.

She was round the corner and out of sight before he'd even finished howling his anger. The rest of the journey was uphill now, but fresh determination powered her. She could do this. Cora's calves ached like they never had before, and her lungs burned in her chest. Bugs, birds and bats flitted from tree to tree, buzzing, screaming, seeking refuge from the flames that were sure to come. Larger mammals burst through the undergrowth from time to time, eyes wide, intent on escape. Above it all, the red in the sky cast its hungry eye on the foothills around her. Knowing she may have made a catastrophic mistake, she pushed on.

Cora crested the last foothill before the outcrop, which rose from the ground like a tooth pushing through a gum. There it was: the murder hole. She sprinted across the last stretch of bare ground and veered right when she reached the familiar tree branch that stood at its base like a headstone. Diving into the small cave, she began to scramble up the narrow chimney that led to higher ground.

Darren, apoplectic, roared in frustration. He hurled a rock, its pitch flat and lethal, right at her, but injury and exhaustion spoiled his aim. The blood was flowing freely down his leg, pumping in and out in dark pulses with his every movement.

"Come on then, big man," she said. "Show me what you've got!"

For a moment, she thought he was going to do it; thought he was going to charge up the chimney, desperate to claim his revenge, but he held back, catching his breath. He turned and surveyed the lands below them, red tongue flicking out. Cora pulled herself over the lip of the ridge and lay there, chest heaving. She felt sick to the guts, but she'd made it. A strange, hoarse choking sound rose up through the chimney, and she risked a quick glance. He was still at the bottom. His shoulders were shaking. Laughter, she realised.

He cast his arm at the thick grey smoke bruising the red horizon. "You're gonna burn anyway."

She had no doubt he was right. Even from her low vantage point halfway up the mountain, she could see flames dancing in the distance and the air was grainy with particulate. Embers fell and smouldered in the detritus. Sparks plumed, motorcycle engines revved furiously and while the cicadas whirred maniacally, not a single bird could be heard above their percussive symphony.

"It looks bad, I'll give you that, but I'll watch you burn first. You're a failure, Darren; a fucking weakling. I've beaten you."

He snarled at this, and hurled another rock. This one cracked off a tree-trunk and fell harmlessly to the ground.

"That's all you've got? You're pathetic."

He roared, long and loud.

"Men like you are all the same. Bullies and cowards. You act like the world owes you something. You think you're a fucking hero, but you're not. You're nothing but a gutless prick."

He bared his teeth at that, his posture shifted into a crouch, then he exploded into action, charging up the chimney.

Cora hefted one of the boulders she kept next to it, and hurled it at him. It bounced past him, but she went again, and caught him fair in the chest. She had to have broken ribs.

Darren fell back, screaming, and she screamed too, in rage and triumph. One after the other, she hurled rocks down at him, giving no quarter, providing no respite. His scales and scutes bent and warped beneath the impact, and he howled wordlessly.

She pictured her boy's bones scattered like broken porcelain, pictured the lizard that had ripped his last breath from him, pictured Sarah, beaten and broken, paddling her feet in the cool water, watching water dragons, pictured Maturin, his little head looking hopefully up at her, still waiting for his breakfast. She stoned Darren like the proverbial ox as the forest fire edged ever closer.

Eventually, he stopped moving. Cora slipped down the scree, unbuckling her knife. She kicked him hard in the stomach, rolling him over onto his back, then rammed the knife into his heart. She half expected him to leap up, to wrench the knife from his chest and lick his life's blood from it, but no—he barely twitched. It was almost disappointing. She wanted to *see* him die.

She twisted the pig-sticker savagely from side to side, hoping to wrench some kind of response from him, but there was nothing. She ripped the blade out with all her might, then buried it deep in his throat. With the same motion she'd used on so many lizards in the past, she rent it open. A gout of arterial blood, warm and redolent arced upwards in a crimson fountain, but still, she wasn't having a repeat of last time; not after everything. She grabbed the machete and drove it across his throat and through the spinal cord, desperate to sever his head. This time he would stay down.

Remembering their moment of unity in the shelter above the waterhole, she grasped his head by the ears and pulled it free. The last strands of scaled skin stretched and snapped, and finally, she cast the dead man's head to the side.

She wanted to collapse, but smoke poured through the clearing below the outcrop now. Flames leapt from tree to tree, and the roaring of the fire drowned out all distant sound. Her lungs burned, leaving her wretched and faint, and she knew there was only one place she wanted to be.

Head swimming, body aching, she stumbled towards the balga trees. They would be loving the fire and would be certain to come back stronger than ever. Such was their nature. Barney's cairn lay there beyond them, and as she wandered, half-blind in the incendiary maelstrom, she relied on muscle memory to find her boy. Everything she'd built and fought for here in this ancient forest was because of him, and now that the flames had doomed her, she had to make it to him before she finally let her mind rest.

When she arrived at the scattered stones, he was there, waiting for her. Barney. Whole again. Cherubic and free, just as she wanted to remember him.

He sat on his cairn and held his arms out to her, and when she came close, he let her kiss him, and hold him tight. She tried to lie down inside the grave. This was their place. It always would be now.

He resisted, wordlessly, refusing to join her.

Cora curled into a ball, cradling the remains that were still cast inside the grave. He spoke then, finally. "Mummy, no. It's time to go." He reached out his hand, and she took it with tears streaking the soot on her thin face. He led her towards a green trail which crept down the opposite end of the balga field.

She recognised it as a goat track she'd rarely used before. The footing was treacherous, but it was her only chance for survival.

Behind her, smoke swirled, and the cicadas, dumb and raucous, burned where they sang. As she took her first tentative steps on the steep path, Barney released her hand and was gone. She had to make this final stretch of the journey without him.

CHAPTER TWENTY

By the time she reached the river, the crackling of the fire had become a deafening roar. Beneath it, she would have sworn the symphonies of hell banged and crashed, but salvation had come regardless. Whether Barney had been real or a figment of her imagination, he'd saved her from the flames. The rest of the job was up to her.

On the riverbank, she saw two people wearing gas-masks and carrying rifles. They stood in the glaring white light of motorcycle headlamps only a few metres from where the kayak and its broken oar still rested. She knew immediately who they were, but she found it incredible they were still here despite the flames.

Embers lit the sky like falling meteorites. Ash settled on Cora's arms and skin as she tried to breathe through the collar of her shirt. She staggered towards the kayak, determined not to let them intervene. She flexed her fingers on the hilt of her knife and snarled, never making eye contact.

One of them raised his gun and told her to stop. He was authoritative but not callous.

"Your friend is dead," Cora said. "Now let me go. There's nothing left here for you."

The other one spoke up. A woman. "We've no friends here. We just look for survivors."

"You're with Black, right?" Cora said. "You're killers, and you're here for Darren. He's dead."

The man muttered something to the woman, and Cora turned to face them at last.

The woman nodded and he lowered his gun.

She stepped forward and offered Cora a gas-mask. "We're with Black, aye, but we're here to help. Looks like you need medical attention, love. Put this on. It'll help with the smoke. As for Darren, the man's scum; we fucked him off a long time ago."

Cora, knowing it was true, and thinking of Sarah, dropped to her knees, racked by sobs.

The woman put an arm around her, hugged her close and pulled the gas-mask over Cora's head. "You've been here a while haven't you? Are you alone? Is there anyone else out here, or is it just you?"

Cora turned back towards the forest. She could hardly see it now. The smoke and the flame were an almost impenetrable wall. It threw heat that washed over them and turned to steam above the river. The kayak would be hot to the touch. None of them could stay here much longer. Through the tears welling in her eyes, she strained to see Barney in her mind once more. If she tried hard enough, she could picture him playing above the swimming hole—but no. He was gone. Time she was too. She shook her head. "It's just me," she said. "I'm all alone. I'm all alone."

"I'm Emily," the woman said. "What's your name?"

Cora doubled over, holding her stomach, cradling her grief. "It's Cora," she said.

"Well, Cora, that's Ruel. I'm going to give you a choice now, but you're going to need to decide quickly. Do you want to come with us? We can get you away from here and see to your wounds. Help you heal – especially if that prick's hurt you."

Cora, barely able to stand, shook her head, bewildered. She had suspected that Sarah's stories didn't add up, but this woman was just saying what she thought Cora wanted to hear. Had to be. No, they couldn't be trusted. Or maybe this was another hallucination, like Barney. Maybe it was her smoke-addled brain trying to lure her back to the forest to die. She staggered past Emily and Ruel, and flipped the kayak. "I won't come with you," she said.

"Wait! We only want to help. You can join our community. You don't have to be alone."

Cora slid the kayak into the water and sat clumsily on the plastic seat. "It sounds nice," she said. "But I can't trust that. I can't trust you. The world doesn't work like that anymore"

She pushed the kayak into the lapping waves, gliding away from Emily and her childish hopes. They begged her to come back, but she paid them no more attention than the burning forest or the grim shape of the mountain behind it, sturdy in the smoke-filled sky. It would endure, and in time, the forests that carpeted its foothills would regenerate. They always did; were in fact supposed to be scoured clean by flame every now and then. With the spirit of Barney living strong in her memory, she too would endure.

Somewhere out there, she would find another place to call home. Her own place, away from the world. For now, though, darkness clogged her mind, just as it did the sky. She had her memories, but her life here was over. She wept as she paddled, her sobs swallowed by the roaring fire. Nothing familiar remained. The very sound of life that had accompanied her existence in this place had vanished. There were no birds, no squabbling bats, and no creatures rustling in the undergrowth. Even, it seemed, the cicadas had fallen silent.

THANK YOU FOR READING

Thank you for taking the time to read this book. We sincerely hope that you enjoyed the story and appreciate your letting us try to entertain you. We realise that your time is valuable, and without the continuing support of people such as yourself, we would not be able to do what we do.

As a thank you, we would like to offer you a free ebook from our range, in return for you signing up to our mailing list. We will never share your details with anyone and will only contact you to let you know about new releases.

You can sign up on our website

http://www.horrifictales.co.uk

If you enjoyed this book, then please consider leaving a short review on Amazon, Goodreads or anywhere else that you, as a reader, visit to learn about new books. One of the most important parts about how well a book sells is how many positive reviews it has, so if you can spare a little more of your valuable time to share the experience with others, even if its just a line or two, then we would really appreciate it.

Thanks, and see you next time!

THE HORRIFIC TALES PUBLISHING TEAM

ABOUT THE AUTHOR

Zachary Ashford was born in Kent in the South-East of England but moved to Australia as a child. He studied creative writing at the University of the Sunshine Coast and teaching at the Queensland University of Technology. He's worked at radio stations, street-press magazines, high schools and construction sites.

Throughout all of that, he's spent an awful lot of time listening to death metal and reading and watching horror fiction. He's a husband and a father, and, if you ask his wife, a big kid at heart. To refute that notion, he's working on another book in his messy study, surrounded by action figures who disagree.

Finally, he's the author of Unnerving Book's *Sole Survivor* novellas, and wants to know how he can get Nick Cage to star in a movie based on one of his stories.

If you figure that out, let him know on twitter or at zacharyashford.com

ALSO FROM HORRIFIC TALES PUBLISHING

High Moor by Graeme Reynolds

High Moor 2: Moonstruck by Graeme Reynolds

High Moor 3: Blood Moon by Graeme Reynolds

Of A Feather by Ken Goldman

Angel Manor by Chantal Noordeloos

Doll Manor by Chantal Noordeloos

Bottled Abyss by Benjamin Kane Ethridge

Lucky's Girl by William Holloway

The Immortal Body by William Holloway

Wasteland Gods by Jonathan Woodrow

Dead Shift by John Llewellyn Probert

The Grieving Stones by Gary McMahon

The Rot by Paul Kane

Deadside Revolution by Terry Grimwood

Song of the Death God by William Holloway

High Cross by Paul Melhuish

Rage of Cthulhu by Gary Fry

The House of Frozen Screams by Thana Niveau

Leaders of the Pack: A Werewolf Anthology

And Cannot Come Again by Simon Bestwick

Scavenger Summer by Steven Savile

A Song for the End by Kit Power

Wild Hunters by Stuart R Brogan

http://www.horrifictales.co.uk

Milton Keynes UK
Ingram Content Group UK Ltd.
UKHW011927140823
426877UK00002B/15

9 781910 283332